Taming Armand

Hayley M. Moon

Published by Hayley Moon, 2024.

This is a work of fiction. Similarities to real people, places, or events are entirely coincidental.

TAMING ARMAND

First edition. February 17, 2024.

Copyright © 2024 Hayley M. Moon.

Written by Hayley M. Moon.

To Darlene and Mary.

Welcome Back and Possibilities

The suit wasn't his style. Normally he stirred clear of such drab and formal colors, but Luca insisted. The older man didn't bother showing him any of the other selections he normally kept in the large trunk he brought to fittings. The Italian stated his father had hand-picked the dark navy blue suit importing the fabric for this special occasion.

Armand wanted to complain but decided against voicing any displeasure with the selection. His father was determined to re-make him in his image. Besides it wouldn't make a difference. Word would get back to his father earning him another strike before he met the man face to face. He watched as Luca frantically brushed at imaginary lint. He, Luca and the others that conceded to his father's authority simply obeyed. No one questioned. Ever.

He rolled his shoulders watching as the fabric moved with him like a second skin. The fit was perfect. Armand couldn't suppress the small smile that formed on his lips. He hadn't expected anything less than perfection from both his father and the man standing to his left. The later had outfitted the family throughout the years himself since he was six.

He caught a glance of Luca's assistant casually sending lustful glances his way in the mirror. Her name slipped him, but their names were always irrelevant.

Armand rolled his eyes smirking as he looked down. It hit him like a freight train; he was back on Alabama soil. A place where he didn't want to be. That thought dragged the corners of upturned lips downward. The anger from earlier at being summoned from the beach front home in Spain returned squashing thoughts of a quick closet fuck.

He took a quick glance at his watch. Armand didn't have much time to gather his thoughts before his glorious appearing. The event was due to start within the hour. He gave Luca a small nod of gratitude; the man slightly bowed before waving his hand in a sweeping motion a signal to all in his party it was time to leave. The assistant lingered clutching the clipboard to her chest. Waiting. She moved along at the cluck of Luca's tongue. His gaze offered a silent apology as they left.

Armand was nearly alone. The tall blond man lurked in his peripheral. He sighed. The Coven's social soirees were out of character for him. Draining. He planned on finding an exit as quickly as possible. He stepped from the platform heading for the elevators. George, Armand's appointed handler for the evening, loomed near since the plane hit the tarmac.

Armand's mind was preoccupied with other matters, and he hadn't given the man much thought until now. A further complication but one he was sure he could deal with. But just like the suit and the party he hadn't been keen on coming back.

Being home brought up too many memories ones he fought to keep suppressed. The women and beautiful Spanish coast allowed him the luxury to forget. As long as the bills were paid, and he could dip into his trust fund for other miscellaneous expenses he hadn't cared about much. Armand attempted to forget about all.

His temple throbbed as thoughts of all of the responsibilities an alpha carried. The ones he would be forced to bare. He shook it off. He didn't want to fall apart; he didn't need to lose himself. Not now.

The key members of the pack would be watching. The Council sizing him up deeming his worthiness. More importantly his father's gaze would be upon him. Scrutinizing. His every word and gesture critiqued. He needed to be ready to perform.

The pressure to fulfill his father's looming expectations were daunting. Armand's palms were sweaty, and he resisted the urge to wipe them on his trousers.

Armand cracked his knuckles as the elevator made it's slow descent to the first floor. Truly, it was time even he couldn't deny it. His time to begin shadowing his father was overdue so had his time to choose a mate. There were many women before he left but none that he would consider elevating to the status of matriarch of their coven.

He knew of the many women that awaited his return his mother told him as much. They were nothing more than vultures waiting for a weakling to come along so they could finish him off. His father told him of the virgins that were waiting for Armand to choose among them. They foolishly believing their purity would strengthen their chances.

The current pool of eligible women proved to be of no challenge to him. He needed the hunt; he craved a chance to seduce. The eldest DuBois desired a woman that wanted him for more than the position he offered. He wanted a mate. Armand was no romantic, but he believed in the old ways and his need for one had grown while in Spain.

Whoever the woman, she would serve as second in command, maintaining order while he was away tending to the multi-billion-dollar empire that served as the backbone of their wealth and power. She would also be the mother and the primary caregiver of their children, so he needed her to be smart as well.

The elevator dinged and he curled his nose up in disgust. The ride down was over all too soon and he remained in the back while George stood in the threshold ensuring the doors remained opened and Armand stayed in his line of sight.

Armand delayed entering the ballroom for as long as was deemed polite even he wasn't above the laws of etiquette. Despite being a room over, he could sense his mother's panic. She was one for decorum and keeping the pack waiting bordered on rudeness. That would not be tolerated, and he sighed. The delay would be something else his father was sure to point out once they were alone. He stole a glance at his watch it was two minutes after the hour the party was scheduled to start.

He paced debating between leaving and entering. He was thirty-two, his parent's first born, and now he was back to claim his birth right. He heard footsteps approach and his head snapped up meeting the cold steely gaze of his father. No words were exchanged but it was clear. It had been less than twenty-four hours, and he was already the source of his father's anger.

Maximillian raised a trimmed eyebrow before turning on his heels leaving his son alone in the room. George resumed his position blocking the opposite door that led to a back hall dashing any plans Armand held of a quick escape.

Time was up. He couldn't wait anymore. It was now. Never was not an option. He squared his shoulders putting stress on the on the stitching.

Slowly, he walked the length of the hall the attendee stopping him at the door telling him to wait for the que to enter. He sighed and bit his tongue holding back the snide remark that was on the tip of it. The young man had placed his hand out the skin of his palm brushing against the middle of his stomach. He didn't like to be touched by the inferiors but brushed it off. He could sense the boy's youth and ignorance and at present wouldn't hold it against him.

It was apparent that his father in his old age had become too friendly and slack. If he had to play this game and forced to become the head he would enforce the old ways ushering in an era of order and respect for the higher ups.

His name was called and immediately he schooled his features appearing bored as he walked into the room. The lights were bright, and he had to look down several times until his eyes adjusted. The applause echoed around him and from the corners of his eyes Armand could see the hungry looks of the women.

The bolder ones started to approach and several touched his arm giving it a slight squeeze while flashing seductive smiles. The young virgins kept their distance only offering demur smiles and playful glances as he passed. Then he saw a woman off to herself, she was the physical embodiment of his mood - bored and annoyed. An older woman was next to her, hands on her hips and at one point gestured in his direction. Armand figured an ambitious mother attempting to sic her daughter on him.

He often wondered if they had any idea what he was capable of no one knew what he had been accused of all those years ago. His father had been careful, the right people had been paid, the body moved in the dead of night. The furniture discarded and the floors cleaned.

During that difficult period, his mother implored her considerable gift of pretending everything was as it were intended, and just like that the matter was no more. It wasn't discussed and his former best friend vanished along with the dead girl's body.

The train of thought was dismissed he didn't need that not now. There was no need to dredge up past unpleasantness.

AMELIA TOSSED BACK another glass. The champagne wasn't particularly good but no doubt expensive not that her delicate palate could distinguish between a bottle of the cheap good stuff and whatever it was she had just swallowed.

For what she needed, which was a quick buzz, it would do. She wanted to leave but her absence would appear disrespectful their alpha had called them all in attendance to welcome back his first-born son.

She rolled her eyes at the conversation that proceeded as her mother held the expensive cotton card stock. Their alpha was gaudy flexing the enormous wealth he had accumulated over the years. She had several protests as to the allocation of the Coven's wealth but had been quickly shushed and dismissed. Diane reminding her the ways of the humans she went to school with were not the ways of their kind.

She looked around the hall at the women standing in anticipation of the soon to be new alpha's arrival. They all had dreams to be chosen. In Amelia's opinion, it was a step back for women and although they shared and could inherit the great wealth of their fathers the women of the Coven possessed little power in comparison to the men. They had no say in the operations of this great and noble experiment.

For Amelia, being the wife of an alpha meant she wouldn't be more than a breeding mare. She refused to be that for any man. The soon to be alpha included. The solution, she would take herself out of the running choosing a quiet corner to watch the fawning of a man that decided to hideaway in Spain for nearly a decade.

A hush descended over the crowd and Amelia turned naturally wanting to capture a glimpse of the man of the hour.

The doors opened revealing him.

He wasn't the same boy she remembered briefly from that summer. He was tall his dark hair the color of freshly poured tar. His stride was long, and he carried himself like a man with purpose, one of great destiny. Her desire was piqued until her gaze landed on his face.

His expression was smug as he looked around the room. She heard several of the recently turned of age girls giggle and she rolled her eyes. She needed another drink and quick.

She waved over a waiter; the young man approached presenting a tray of freshly poured glasses. Amelia had barely raised her arm when she felt a firm hand on her wrist. It was her mother and she sighed disappointed that she wouldn't be able to chase her buzz.

Diane wore a disapproving frown and raised her eyebrows. Amelia sighed and quickly dropped her hand to her side. The waiter gave a slight nod before leaving the two women.

"Yes, Mother?" The smile was forced, and Diane moved to stand in front of her daughter.

"You've had enough. Now come let me introduce you to Armand; he's handsome, isn't he? Not to mention tall."

Her mother sucked her teeth, "which is good for you."

Amelia leaned forward fighting the urge to hunch over, "he's okay, I guess as far as arrogant assholes go. I don't want to meet him. So, don't waste your time."

"Nonsense. Watch your language and your tone he will be the new alpha fairly soon." Diane looked around and roughly took hold of her daughter's upper arm leading her to a vacant area. The majority of the attendees had formed a circle around the guest of honor. The women vying to catch his eye, the men hoping to gain favor and become part of the inner circle once he was crowned.

"Mother please. That hurts." She whispered trying to pull free of Diane's grasp.

"Enough!" Diane hissed at her oldest.

"Amelia, you are not only our eldest child but our only daughter. You have obligations to this family. Now, a match between you and Armand wouldn't that be something. Just think of all of the changes and ideas you have. You would have a direct line to the top, no one would ignore those..." Diane looked around twirling her index finger as she sought for the appropriate word.

"Petitions?" Amelia tired of waiting filled in the silence.

"Yes, those things," the older woman snapped, "now think of that. He," she gestured toward the crowd, "could help tremendously, now as I was saying. It's time you two were introduced."

Her mother wore that smile that warned everyone close to her that she was up to something, and it involved you.

"Does Father know that you are trying to pawn me off like this?"

"Yes, he does. Your father is in full agreement. It is time you marry; and just think a marriage between the two of you would further elevate this family. We would be untouchable. You would be the most powerful woman here, and your children..." she shook her head eyes closed, "I would be the grandmother of a future alpha."

Diane opened her eyes the smile was sly with the tips of eggshell white canines peeking beneath a crimson-stained top lip.

Amelia laughed, "what makes you think he is interested in marrying?"

"He doesn't have a choice." She hissed looking around making sure that what she was about to say next wouldn't be overheard.

"He's dying." She whispered.

Amelia's eyes widened and she looked toward the front of the crowd, "he's so young, wow. That's so sad, horrible even and here I am thinking the worst of him."

For a moment, the young woman started to grow solemn instantly regretting all of the ill thoughts she had of him and the family.

Diane rolled her eyes, "no, not him. His father. That's why he's back but I am pretty sure Maximillian hasn't told him yet," she pointed her finger in Amelia's face, "don't tell anyone. If one word of this gets out your father will be in such trouble."

She was taking a huge risk mentioning it there in the mist of the members but given that everyone seem enthralled with Maximillian's eldest she felt pretty confident what she said would remain secret.

Her gaze was hard, it was one her mother rarely used but when she did if left no question, she meant business. Amelia had to look away from her mother's penetrating glare.

The look from before was back and Diane wore a sly smile as she wrapped her arm around Amelia's and started to lead her toward the crowd.

After a little maneuvering on Diane's part, they had worked their way up the line to the very front. Diane gave Amelia a small pat of reassurance on her lower back as he approached.

Armand saw her the moment he walked into the room. She hadn't swarmed him like the others, and he found her attempts of being disinterested endearing. It was a first that a woman hadn't sought him out. Relations that started that way didn't last long but Armand didn't put up much of a fight. He played the game had his fun then discarded them.

She was tall, lean with an hourglass figure. Her curves were soft and the way her golden skin captured the light gave the appearance of an evening sunset. He couldn't help but take notice of her ample chest. The dress was simple but hugged her frame. It wasn't too revealing like the other gowns, if one could call them such, that he had seen this evening. Class was the only word he could use to describe her. In this woman he saw a potential mate and he took note to ask his mother about her.

He watched from the corner of his eye as an older woman practically dragged her to the line that had begun to form. Everyone made their introductions as he made his way around the large circle, his desire started to grow the closer he came to her.

She wanted to bolt for the door or the nearest corner. He was about a foot away and Amelia had to lock her knees. It was near her time of the month and her heighten sense of smell only added to the desire for him. Her belly flipped as she watched him shake her mother's hand his gaze on her as he spoke soft salutations.

"Welcome home; it's so good to have you back Armand. This is my eldest, Amelia."

At the sound of her name she slowly brought her gaze from his chest and up to meet his dark hazel eyes.

She stopped breathing.

Words failed him as the greeting he had practiced on the flight and repeated several times tonight escaped him. She was even more stunning up close, and he resisted the urge to caress her cheek.

Diane's smile was wide as she looked from her daughter to Armand. She lightly cleared her throat causing Amelia to involuntarily giggle and Armand to stutter.

"Hello." Amelia spoke softly her eyes never leaving his.

"Hello." He took her hand squeezing it firmly but gently, "I'm glad you could make it this evening."

"I'm..." the words died on her tongue.

His gaze was intense. Hypnotic. She looked away feeling uncomfortable with how her body was responding to him.

She cleared her throat, "Same." She removed her hand from his. The moment gone.

He stood staring at her not wanting to leave. She met his gaze once again before a young blonde came close and stared silently bullying her way in.

"I hope to see more of you, Amelia." He bowed slightly and she blushed.

He focused his attention on the blonde. Diane gently led her daughter away the look on her face was of absolute joy.

THE EVENING PASSED slowly, and Armand would casually glance around the room searching for her. He had planned to make his way to speak with her again but kept being pulled away by the desperate and power-hungry young women blocking his path.

By the time he had untangled himself from their snares and that of their mother's she was gone. He wasn't sure why but upon discovering she had left he became angry. He started dismissing people, his tone sharp and the well-rehearsed words were biting causing murmurs that weren't missed by his parents.

After the three-hour mark, the welcome home party started to thin out. Only a few of the stragglers remained, mostly women looking for a quick lay with the future alpha.

His young brother Caesar approached with a small smirk on his face. The two embraced briefly before separating with Caesar stepping back.

"It's not often a god comes down from Olympus to mingle with us mere mortals. What brought you back brother?"

"Father." Armand breathed, and Caesar simply nodded.

"Of course. Kronos summoning back Zeus. Be sure you don't get devoured." Caesar chuckled before leaving Armand to his thoughts as he followed the last few members toward the exit.

Armand noted two sisters standing. They were watching him and whispering; he debated taking them back to his room, but his father came into view before he had made his decision. The old man was rapidly approaching a scowl etched into his chiseled and well-aged face. Once again his needs would have to wait. The idea of a quick fuck forgotten.

"Upstairs, now." His father growled as he passed not bothering to slow down.

HE ENTERED THE PENTHOUSE to find his mother waiting for him. She hugged him tight, and he couldn't help but laugh. Hemesh pushed him at arm's length before bringing her hands down to her sides.

"I am so glad you are home son," her smile was warm, eyes soft. Armand knew what was next and he steeled himself for the verbal assault that was guaranteed to follow.

"Armie, why were you so rude tonight?" She looked puzzled and he looked away to avoid rolling his eyes at his childhood nickname.

His father only stood a few feet away his eyes shifting from dark blue to a deep hazel.

"Mother."

She held up her hand cutting him off.

"I painstakingly gathered the most prominent families and the most eligible, beautiful and many of them virgins here for you tonight. Your behavior was not that of the eldest child an eldest son at that."

She sighed turning and heading over to the small lounge.

"Sit."

Armand sat next to her on the small sofa crossing one leg over the other. They sat in silence a moment before he spoke.

"Where is Hera? I spoke with Caesar earlier, he seems well." He looked around hoping he sounded sincere.

Hemesh smiled, "we both know you are not interested in the happenings and whereabouts of your brother and sister. But since you asked. Hera is studying for finals and your brother closed a very large account. You know he came in from London to see you. He wanted to welcome you home and to bring you up to speed. I'm sure you'd like to know he's getting married later this year."

His eyebrows shot up in surprise, "wow, why didn't anyone call?" His tone was dull, and he uncrossed his legs.

"We tried. You are a hard man to get a hold of darling and I grew weary of leaving messages with your assistant." His mother stated giving him the look he dreaded, which meant she called once didn't get the desired outcome and never called again.

Maximilian approached and sat in the chair opposite the pair.

"Tonight was about you, and you lost your head. No focus and that worries me, but Caesar will by your side he'll bring you up to speed rather quickly," his father stated quietly.

Armand sighed he tried not to sound agitated, "how so, Father? This was your and Mother's little soiree, I came. I mingled. I have done more than fulfill my social obligation this evening. Besides I don't need to be brought up to speed. Caesar can return to London I don't need a babysitter." He stated rubbing his hands together.

His father ignored him waving his hand.

"That girl you kept staring at Amelia. She's from a good family; she's older around your age which is good for you. You need a woman more into her own. Shall I reach out to her father, Charles? I can start the necessary introductions."

Maximilian was torn, he wanted his son to fulfill his duty but not like this. He was reluctant to force the match.

Armand almost balked, "what?! I was unaware Father that this was a betrothal gala," he said through clenched teeth.

The patriarch waved his hand, "one in the same, you are well aware of our ways. Tonight was your introduction, ten years late but better late than never. I managed to find a more than adequate match for your brother and soon will do the same for Hera. The Beta of the Westland Coven of Russia has expressed interest", he paused eyeballing his eldest, "do you understand what is happening? We must move fast."

His father motioned for his valet holding up his empty glass.

"Your mother and I let you go off and be on your own for a while thinking that once this phase of yours was over that you'd return ready to claim your place and assume your responsibility."

His father regarded him a moment before taking the glass of scotch from the tall slender man.

"Now, I noticed the young woman that caught your eye. Her name's Amelia sweet woman very smart from what I hear. Which is a huge asset and an upgrade from the whores you frequent. We think she'd be a good fit for you," he gestured toward his eldest with his glass, "she's beautiful, Amelia would make a fine wife."

"She's from a good family, with strong roots in the coven. A founding family." His mother stated nodding at him expectantly.

Armand wanted to snarl, he hadn't returned to take part in his parents' mating games and before he left discussed at length of his brother taking the mantle of alpha in his place. He would gladly step aside with no fanfare. That evening both parents listened intently. His mother's thin lips slightly downturned. His father's expression unreadable.

It was only after he had nervously pleaded his case that his old man laughed him out of the room. Armand closed his eyes shaking his head slightly a loose chocolate curl falling onto his forehead.

"She's attractive but there were many women there so she kind of blended in," he stated quickly. He was afraid to continue as well as refused to acknowledge the heat that stirred in his belly. He looked down at the tip of his polished loafer.

Hemesh smiled at her husband.

Maximillian raised his eyebrows before schooling his features. It seemed he wouldn't have to do much pushing. His son was like him in many respects and if this woman was something he wanted. There was no doubt he would go after her.

Armand's interest would be a great benefit as he needed his son to choose the girl. Their fate and the legacy of their lineage depended on it. His face became hard once again as he brought the crystal glass to his lips and took a long sip.

Hopefully, their union would ensure his secrets were safe.

DIANE SLID ACROSS THE warm leather seat next to her daughter. Her smile would have lit their path on the twenty minute drive home. Armand noticed her daughter. Diane wouldn't mention it, but she noticed Amelia's gaze drifting to the young man as well. So had the others especially the young women. It was hard not to notice their soon to be alpha's lingering glance on the five eleven mocha skinned beauty.

It would be wise for them all to be careful especially them. Their alpha as well as the DuBois family had many enemies and would exploit any weakness. Amelia was a target now with Armand's attention she would be seen as competition. The Anaheim matriarch was unaware how large of a target her daughter would become.

Diane cast a sideways glance at her eldest during the long ride. The attention she received from Armand was valuable, the young woman's stock would drastically rise making her highly sought after by the eligible males of their pack.

Her mind raced as she formulated a list in her head. She wouldn't be a proper mother if she didn't have contingencies in case things fell through with Armand. Diane wasn't as convinced as her husband that Maximillian would make good on his promise.

Amelia was staring out the window her hands folded delicately in her lap. She refused to discuss the party, Armand nor her response to his presence. She knew her mother noticed, and this only added to her annoyance. Her body reacted in an unusual way at the thought of him and she wasn't sure if she was ready to accept it.

Not just yet.

If not tonight, then in the morning at the breakfast table her family would gang up on her. They would ask questions and make suggestions on how to snag a man. It would be another morning of her widowed aunt tapping her thigh with the butt of a small amber vial. She had a collection of them lined along her bookcase. She was giddy but bit down on her tongue to stop the laughter bubbling up inside. Amelia wanted to laugh but any sign of joy would be an invitation for her mother to speak. Instead she sat silently and continued to stare out the window her eyes sharp as she spotted small rodents peeking from behind the leafy branches of the large Oaks lined along the driveway.

Diane wanted to speak but decided against it as much as it pained her she remained silent. But the long drive home had given her much time to start mentally laying the groundwork for the plan.

Amelia had his attention and that was a start. The issue arose was whether her daughter could keep it.

The young man was rebellious and when it came to women had the attention span of a gnat. Diane speculated extreme matters would have to be taken. She would have to gather the maids and grounds keepers.

Since Armand had taken an interest, others that had previously passed Amelia over would come calling.

She ran her eyes over the young woman next to her, she would need a new wardrobe something different than the flare legged jeans, t-shirts and oversized cardigans that had become the young woman's signature.

Diane shook her head that would not do.

The white limo came to a stop and before Alonso could make it around to their side of the car, Amelia was out and halfway up the stairs to the front door.

Diane slide across the leather seat her four-inch stilettos placed firmly on the driveway. She thanked Alonso as she slowly headed up the stairs her mind shifting to earlier tonight and the looks shared between the two stubborn wolves.

She entered the foyer the temporary high gone. Her smile faded as she closed the door locking it behind her. Every move counted now, and she would speak with Hemesh. She needed to know whether to push Amelia closer in the young man's direction or detour her all together. She hoped for the former; a marriage and alliance such as theirs would bring great prestige to the Anaheim clan ensuring their linage remained connected to the alpha.

AMELIA COULDN'T EXPLAIN it, but her heart raced, and her palm still tingled where his large hand held hers.

She went to her bathroom and stood in front of the large floor length mirror. Slowly, she peeled the gown down her long arms pushing it slowly down her torso and over her hips. It fell in a puddle around her ankles, and she stepped out of the circle, and using her left foot kicked it to the side.

Her body was flushed, and she fingered the lace panties lightly tugging at the delicate fabric. Her nipples harden becoming little brownish peaks that peered through the flesh tone lace.

Amelia noted this was a first.

Her body had never been so unruly.

DIANE ENTERED THE MASTER suite to find her husband on his laptop reclined against the headboard. She smiled glad to see him awake to relay the news and discuss the possibilities.

Charles looked at his wife over the rim of his glasses his brown eyes shining with anticipation.

"So, how was it? Did he notice her?"

Diane made her way around the bed and sat next to him. Her full lips slowly parted into a smile, as she nodded vigorously.

"Yes, he's stubborn and has an amazing poker face by the way but I could tell. He's interested but," her expression fell, and she looked away, "he's temperamental." She brought her gaze to rest on him.

"It could simply be lust." She added unsure of herself for the first time that night.

Charles chuckled closing the laptop; he peeled off his glasses and looked at her.

"It doesn't matter. Either way I have made it clear to Max that Armand must choose Amelia. It's that simple."

Diane looked at him sharply, "remember dear this is Maximillian DuBois nothing is ever 'simple' with that man." She sighed, "do you think you may have pushed too far?" Diane was starting to worry putting the two wolves in each other's path and letting fate guide the way was much different than making demands of their alpha.

The middle aged woman knew her husband was playing with fire just as he always had but with one miscalculated step they would all burn.

Charles set the laptop aside and moved closer to his wife. He placed a large hand on the side of her face gently stroking her bottom lip with his calloused thumb.

"You worry too much darling. He owes me everything. Now, I couldn't become alpha, but I can make sure that our grandchild does. We will always have a tie, a blood tie. With Amelia as the Coven's matriarch think of the influence we will have. Finally, we can make the changes necessary not to mention we'll have the head of the coven in our backpocket."

Diane sighed there was no convincing him otherwise although she would love for nothing more than her oldest to bag their most eligible bachelor she would not risk her daughter in the process.

Charles brought his hand to her chin raising her head up so their eyes met.

"This will go well. Max has agreed to do his part we just have to make sure she is ready. There's where you come in."

Diane started to protest but was cut off by Charles raising his hand.

"At a certain point she will need to know that as the eldest she has certain duties to this family."

Diane sighed, "I will make sure she is ready I will need to spend quite a bit of money. She will need a new wardrobe; hair, nails the usual if she is to compete and look presentable when she's chosen."

She picked at the covers looking away before bringing her gaze back to rest on him.

"If this all falls apart, if Max decides he no longer wants to honor the agreement, I know," she placed her hand on Charles' chest as he was about to interject, "it won't but we always have to be prepared. If this falls apart, Max will come for us, they all will."

Charles looked deep into her eyes, "I won't let that happen."

He kissed her forehead. Diane closed her eyes she hoped so.

Discussions and The End

Hemesh and Maximillian talked quietly of the evening's festivities, their son only gave brief answers opting to listen to his parents' banter. He hoped the small talk would end soon so he could leave.

His phone buzzed in his blazer pocket. Armand didn't' bother removing the phone. There was no need to check the ID at this hour Armand knew it could only be one person, Camille.

He wasn't sure how she knew he was stateside. She wasn't at the party but that wouldn't stop him from meeting her and having his needs sated.

Armand made his excuses citing an early morning meeting to discuss business in Europe as the reason for his premature departure. He bent down and placed a kiss on his mother's cheek and with a final nod to his father left. He only pulled the phone from his pocket once he was shrouded in the glass cage of the elevator.

The attendant motioned for his colleague when the alpha's eldest stepped from the elevator. In what could only be counted as seconds the black Lamborghini was out front the suicide door up and without as much as a glance toward the two men Armand slide onto the maroon leather and sped off into the night.

The small talk ceased as soon as Hemesh and Maximillian were assured their son was out of ear shot. The older man sighed bringing his free hand up as a sign of dismissal to his personal valet. John bowed before swiftly leaving the room and in the direction of the servants' floor.

Hemesh stood and walked over to the large window overlooking the city.

"Do you think he'll choose her?" She asked playing with the large solitaire sapphire at the base of her collarbone.

Maximillian slowly stood thinking of an answer. He poured another drink before joining her by the window.

"I don't know. We can nudge him in her direction but it's up to Diane and Charles to keep the girl in his path. Amelia must hold his attention."

The slender Indian woman stared at his reflection her dark eyes meeting his deep blues.

"Armand, doesn't like to be nudged." She turned to face him, "you know that."

Maximillian looked away. He sighed bringing his shoulders back as he brought his eyes back to rest on hers.

"Well, we have to try, he must choose the girl."

"Why?" Her tone was defeated as her eyes pleaded with those of her husband's.

He swallowed the liquor in one large gulp.

"You know why." They both knew no explanation was needed.

She sighed dropping her hands to her sides, she did know and that is what bothered her.

"That's his price Hemesh."

He started in the direction of their bedroom Hemesh followed closely behind. In the master suite he placed the empty glass on the dresser with a thud and started to undo his tie. His wife kicked off her heels leaving them near the door as she approached the chaise lounge at the foot of the bed.

"What do you mean his price Max? He's been paid many times over."

He ripped the tie from his neck throwing it to the floor.

"Well, that hasn't been enough."

"He runs the council as well as sits at the Table of Selene, the only person in the Coven aside from yourself to occupy a seat at both tables. What more could he want?"

"A blood tie." he shouted turning toward her.

Hemesh didn't flinch at the outburst; he was angry; he didn't like when someone else had the upper hand.

"He wants his daughter with our son. That's his price. He not only helped but played an integral part in my being here as alpha."

He sat beside her slowly reaching for her hand.

"He has proof. He is the last living witness and if that were to get out we're done. All of us; you, Armand, Hera, Caesar. They wouldn't let any of you live. I couldn't bear loosing you and the kids. This is my fault I was foolish, but Samuel, he was leading us down a dark path something had to be done."

She gave his hand a light squeeze, but Hemesh would offer no sympathy tonight she had none.

"Yes, but your son has to pay for your sin. How's that fair my love?"

He looked up at her.

"It isn't but he must do what is required of him. If he doesn't choose the girl of his own free will then I will betroth them, and he will wed her regardless."

Maximillian stared at the far wall.

"You are going to force your son to marry a woman he possibly does not or cannot love?"

He sighed, "if I must."

"So, you want him to be like us?"

He looked at her, "we aren't that bad Hemesh. You weren't my first choice, but I have kept my word. You have fulfilled your duties. You have been more than adequate as a wife and partner."

She chuckled, "you're not so bad yourself."

She sighed squeezing his hand, "but I wanted things to be different for them. All of them. Especially Armand. He's sensitive although he works very hard not to show it."

Max placed a kiss on her forehead, "he's the first-born son. We don't have options not in our world."

He stood his wife offering him a soft smile as their hands slowly parted. She watched as he disappeared into the bathroom.

The Coven's matriarch was defeated but recalling how her son had watched the young woman, and the small glances Amelia threw his way, a flame of hope burned. Hemesh decided she would do a little nudging of her own. She would implore the help of her second son, Caesar.

ARMAND WOKE WITH AMELIA on his mind. His thoughts went to the night before and of Camille riding him hard. He couldn't help but throw his head back eyes closed as he focused on images of Amelia; he came twice fantasizing that she was the one above him.

He sighed annoyed; his mood shifted to confusion then disappointment when he realized it was the blonde snuggled against his side. Quickly he sat up jostling the young woman from her slumber. Camille stirred before lazily rising into a sitting position. She didn't bother covering her chest.

"Are you late for something?" She asked rising onto her knees as she pressed her bare chest into his muscled back.

He rolled his eyes her desperation was always a source of annoyance. He was confused as to why she had remained in his bed.

"No, I'm confused."

She giggled girlishly, "maybe I can help," she whispered seductively in his ear before bringing her arms around his chest. The grip on her wrist was hard causing her to stop.

"Come on," she moved her free hand down his stomach toward his groin.

Roughly he pushed it away and abruptly stood nearly causing her to fall off the bed.

She sat back pulling the lose sheet around herself looking at him.

"What's wrong?"

"I am trying to understand, why are you still here?"

Armand sighed as he looked down at her his full lips turned downward. His nose upturned slightly. Camille recoiled at the disgust expressed. She clinched the sheet tighter.

"Armand, what are you talking about? You wanted me here."

"No Camille, I wanted you here last night to fuck. Afterwards you leave, what part of that don't you understand?"

"I have a meeting this morning by the time I'm done with my shower I want you gone."

His voice was low. Deadly.

Her shoulders dropped. Camille recoiled at the chilliness of his tone. Armand ignored the defeated expression and headed for the shower. If he would have stayed he would have chastised her for the watery wide eyed gaze.

Camille wanted to dismiss his words and attribute them to his infamous mood shifts but she could no longer fool herself into believing that she had a piece of his heart. It was clear he only called when he needed someone beautiful on his arm or a body in his bed. Armand was a prince in their world, and they all were there to serve in whatever capacity deemed fit for the occasion.

She rose dressing in no hurried fashion and sat on the edge of the California king waiting until he finished.

Armand let the hot water cascade down his back leaving red angry skin in their wake. The steam caused beads of sweat to rise on his forehead. Once again Amelia occupied his thoughts and an indescribable need surged through him causing his cock to rise at an angle the tip nearly touching his belly button.

His desire quickly turned to anger at how the mere thought of this mousy woman reduced him to a horny teenager. Armand senses kicked in gear as he focused. He could hear movement in the bedroom obviously Camille hadn't gotten the message.

At the mere mention thought of her his cock went limp. Forcefully he gripped the handles turning them until the water stop. He left indentations on the gold finishes.

He dried entering his bedroom nude to find Camille in the spot where he had left her only now she was clothed in the bodycon dress she had worn from the previous night's afterparty.

She was angry. Armand hissed ignoring her as he went to the large walk in closet. He dressed and entered the bedroom stopping a few feet in front of her.

Camille sat staring at her platforms.

"I thought I made it clear I wanted you out by the time I finished." Her lack of obedience was another reason he would impose harsher punishments. This was another sign his father had become too lenient.

She slowly looked up at him.

"Do you care about me Armand? Like ever?"

He rolled his eyes at Camille's antics.

Armand despised weak women, and wondered how Amelia would have responded. He quickly dismissed the notion fearing his body's response. He didn't want Camille to get the wrong impression.

"No, I don't. Not ever."

His revelation went straight to her heart and Camille lunged at him like a wild cat her beaded clutch high in the air. He easily caught her hand while wrapping the other around her neck. He spun them around Camille's back crashing against the floor to ceiling glass window.

Armand was enraged. Using his body to hold her in place. She was immobile. He snarled his pupils narrowing into slits. His chiseled features somewhere between animal and man. A lesser wolf would have recoiled in fear.

Camille felt the tips of claws piercing the delicate skin of her neck and wrist. She could resist, fight back but she didn't. Instead she chose to relax against the glass. If Armand wanted to kill her then she would acquiesce to the man she had freely given her body to over the years. Even in his absence she waited. Armand would always hold a piece of her heart.

He smirked as the fire in her eyes dimmed before it was extinguished. Armand knew he had her full surrender when her body sagged against his. Armand released her and stepped back watching as she slid to the floor. The t-shirt clung to his aching muscles as he fought the shift. His body damp from the mental exhaustion.

Armand watched as she rose using the glass as support. Camille stood her spine straight and shoulders back causing her collar bone to be more pronounced. She stared at him.

His breathing returned to normal as he stood prepared for her to lunge at him again. He followed her movements as she slowly stooped down picking up the discarded handbag. The surrender he witnessed earlier in those large green doe eyes was gone replaced by something dark. Primal.

If she had been a man he would have taken the lingering contact as a challenge. He would have killed her without a second thought. His only regret would be staining the antique wooden floors he sourced from Chile.

"You're going to regret this Armand," Camille whispered.

His shoulders began to rise and fall as he let out a laugh that was absorbed by the matte black velvet wallpaper.

Tension left his body as he headed to the walk in, "whatever you say Camille." He through the line over his shoulder as he disappeared for a second time into the large closet.

Camille left on wobbly legs. Her mind raced. She entered the elevator thinking to her knowledge Armand had no weakness aside from his arrogance. Nevertheless she would find one.

Thinking of You

Amelia woke to a stream of sunlight across her face and the smell of breakfast downstairs. She decided to get up and try to beat her brothers to the table for once. She went to the private bathroom to shower. As the hot water cascaded down her body, her mind shifted to Armand and the way he stalked around the room.

"Arrogant prick." She lathered the loafer and brought it over her body hurrying as the thought of breakfast overtook her thoughts. She finished quickly, dressed and headed downstairs.

Amelia scoffed when she saw everyone was present. She had an odd feeling her family had been waiting for her.

"Amelia," her dad stood smiling, "come in daughter, sit."

Diane took a quick sip from her large mug before sitting it down her eyes never once leaving the young woman.

"Ok," Amelia sat next to her great aunt, the woman cast her one eye over at her disapprovingly before rolling it and crossing her arms.

Charles sat down folding the napkin in his lap.

"The woman of the hour."

"Dad, what's this about?"

"You my girl and..." he hesitated his eyes going wide with excitement, "Armand."

One of her brothers howled the other looked at her wiggling his eyebrows.

"Who would have thunk it, our dear sweet, nerdy," Liam was cut off by Mason.

"Boring," Mason sang out.

Liam continued, "yes boring Amelia could pull a future Alpha, whoohoo!" He clapped falling backward in this chair, Mason joined in the dramatics clutching his chest.

"Both of you stop it," Diane hissed, "your sister is not boring." She turned her attention to her daughter.

"But Amelia we will need to spice things up a bit. Clear your schedule; today we are going shopping."

Amelia looked around, "I can't believe this, he and I barely spoke a minute, so I don't know what everyone is all excited about."

"My dear it was the interaction," her mother cut in her hands clasped under her chin.

Her aunt mumbled something indistinguishable under her breath. Mason sensed his aunt's displeasure and goaded her.

"What's that Aunt Nancy? Do you not approve of Amelia's new beau?"

"He's nothing but trouble. That whole family are nothing but liars," the woman spat her large grey, hazy eyes landing on them all. It was rumored their great aunt was blind but moved around the large home with ease.

Diane cut her off causing the older woman to growl low in her throat usually her aunt was the first to try and push her toward matrimony but now the woman seemed dead set against even mentioning it.

Amelia wouldn't push her aunt at least not in front of her family she would seek her out later.

"Shopping for what exactly Mother?" The young woman continued to stare at her mother.

"Clothes, shoes, the works. Your hair needs a touch up. I understand your studies are important darling but don't let your looks go to hell. Now," she sighed heavily, "with Armand's eye on you that means the rest of the pack will also be watching and other eligible bachelors will be calling each trying to make their claim before Armand does."

She leaned back in the chair and chuckled, "it's all so exciting!"

THE MEETING WAS APPROACHING the two hour mark. Armand tuned out the monotone voice of the middle aged CFO as he drawled on about the company's projected profits for the upcoming quarter.

It was nearly as boring as Jason's presentation on company culture. Armand didn't see the need for the formalities, the company was turning a profit their EBDITA was strong so a fifteen-minute meeting or better yet, an email would have sufficed.

But his brother was insistent that he be brought up to speed on the company before he would step aside and leave the day-to-day operations to Armand. It was another one of their Father's requests he would have to fulfill.

Slowly, he angled his chair toward the large window overlooking the city skyline. He was about to turn around bored with the dull and ditzy looking freshman walking past until he saw her.

She was walking with a group of teens. One in particular was talking animatedly. Amelia like the rest of the group had on jeans except hers were two sizes too big with a belt and cardigan.

The image before him was a sharp contrast to the one two nights ago. She was covered and Armand let out a hiss at being deprived of the site of the woman's creamy flesh. He vowed to uncover more. His desire to know this woman was strong.

The group stopped at the crosswalk the sun glistening on Amelia's chocolate locs and Armand had a sudden urge to touch them. He wanted to relish in their texture, but most importantly he wanted to touch her. He crossed his legs as he felt himself react.

Gerald had taken his boss' hiss as a sign of displeasure with the presentation stopping mid-sentence to stare at him.

Caesar watched Armand crane his neck until he could no longer see her from his vantage point. Armand sighed before turning back to the room to find several pairs of eyes on him including his kid brother who sported an amused expression.

"Continue Gerald," Armand stated through clenched teeth.

The grey haired man nodded before nervously turning to the slides his hand high in the air as he pointed at peaks and graphs.

Caesar continued to stare at his brother the corners of his lips turned upward revealing straight white teeth.

Armand stared ahead annoyed he had been caught. He was pretty sure their mother informed his brother as well as his sister of Amelia.

At the conclusion of the presentation, Caesar directed the team to take a break; hurriedly they rose exiting the room ready to the leave the brothers' imposing presence.

When the last person left, Armand angled his foot so the tip of his shoe was pointed outward and kicked Caesar in the shin.

"Ouch, what was that for?"

Armand only answered by giving him the bird. Caesar chuckled as he rubbed his leg, "that's going to leave a bruise."

"Good." Armand stated attempting to angle his body toward the window hoping to catch another glimpse of Amelia.

Caesar took note of this and smiled.

He reached out grabbing his brother's shoulder, "how about lunch, my treat."

"I have plans." Armand stated not bothering to look at him.

"Such as?"

Armand turned his attention now on his brother before returning his gaze back to the street below.

"Exactly. Let's go."

It was only minutes later that Armand was in the passenger seat of his brother's Porsche as the two made their way to *Argentine's*.

Caesar cut in and out of traffic smiling, part of him glad to have his brother home the other amused as he had never seen him like this.

"What are you smiling about?" he asked frustrated mostly at the other's driving.

"You, I've never seen you like this over a woman."

Armand sighed, "like what? I'm doing nothing."

"Amelia." Caesar enunciated the word the smile never leaving his lips.

"Did Mother tell you about the conversation last night?"

The driver started laughing, "of course she did. I'm going to help you. From what I know about Amelia I think she'll be perfect for you."

Armand was quiet for several seconds before he asked softly, "you know her?"

"In a casual sense. The bleeding heart type. She heads up a non-profit for low-income girls we donate you know nice tax write off."

More silence. Caesar knew his brother was curious but wouldn't ask any questions.

"Well, Amelia is a student I think she's working on a Ph.D. in History or art something like that."

A slight humph was Armand's only response.

At the red light, Caesar stole a glance at his brother he was still staring out the window.

"Well, she has a great body. Since you're not interested I wouldn't mind chatting her up you know? Maybe giving her a roll in the hay before I tie the knot." He stated jokingly.

This got Armand's attention as he now faced his brother, "leave her alone. Besides I thought you were into Evelyn."

The smile on his face turned devilish as he hit the gas, "I am but I can still have a little fun here and there." He chuckled as he pulled the car in front of the valet stand the two got out heading into the restaurant.

The hostess side stepped the couple she was assisting and approached them.

"Your usual, sir?" she asked Caesar as she ran her eyes up and down Armand's body.

Caesar cleared his throat capturing the young woman's attention. He had become uncomfortable with being ignored.

"Yes," he leaned in reminding the two he was present. His intrusion clearly annoying the hostess.

"This way," her voice flirtatious as she led them toward a private area reserved for some of the town's more elite to conduct business over a good meal and away from the general diners.

"The waiter will be with you shortly; is there anything else I can get you?" She looked down through heavy lids at Armand her tone implying more than what was on the menu.

The eldest DuBois gestured casually as if he was shushing away a fly, "no that's all." He responded without looking.

Caesar watched as her face fell and cheeks flushed before whispering, "have a good lunch," before hurrying to her post.

"You could have at least looked at her." Caesar watched the woman walk away until she was out of sight.

Armand stared over the menu at his brother, "that's the problem, you feel too much." He returned his gaze back to the entree options.

"How's the fiancé?" he spat out the word as if it tasted sour.

"She's fine; you are coming to my wedding dear best man?"

"Do I have a choice?"

"I suppose not. Well, look at it this way, if your feelings toward Amelia are as strong as I sense they are we could have a double wedding. Mother would be overjoyed. Next, we just need to strong arm Hera somehow and who knows maybe we could do a three for one."

He wiggled his eyebrows. Armand folded his menu and playfully smacked his brother in the head with the stiff leather.

They both laughed before the two fell silent.

"Oddly enough, I've missed this."

"Me too." Armand admitted.

The waiter arrived taking the pair's drink order. Caesar ordered a bourbon Armand followed suit requesting his neat. The dark-skinned man nodded before disappearing in the direction of the bar.

"Brother, why did you come back so soon? Not that I am complaining, but I must say I thoroughly enjoyed being the only son in town. I have all of Mother's affections but I'm curious you seemed hell bent on going on this adventure. I figured you would be gone for at least two more years."

Armand sighed leaning forward placing his elbows on the table. He looked solemn.

"I told you before, Father. He called said I needed to come earlier than expected, that it was time." He leaned back waving his hands in the air. He pinched the bridge of his nose.

"I doubt if you answered the phone. It's all Mother could talk about."

Armand rolled his eyes smirking, "okay he left a very long voice mail or rather several stitched together voice mails."

Caesar raised an eyebrow.

"Okay, they were left with my assistant but still, I got them. I listened to them. That's beside the point."

"Well, it is the point. I mean Dad was what twenty-five when he took over the Coven. Technically, you are overdue bud, what are you thirty..." he paused playfully counting on his fingers.

Armand swatted at his hand.

"Maybe he wants you to take the mantle. Become King, so to speak. With his oversight, I'm sure."

"By the decree I can only become alpha if he dies and he looks alive and well. Very fit and strong so, I think it was a ploy to get me back in town so they could force one of these women on me. Mother has been hinting at grandchildren since I got back."

"Ahh, don't forget brother the decree also states if the leader steps aside. Maybe he wants to retire, move to Florida."

"Very funny," Armand paused and regarded his brother, "you know before I left I advocated on your behalf. You are better suited for this alpha business more so than I am. Besides I don't want it. I've made it very clear."

Armand picked up the tri fold, "I think I'll go with steak." He let it fall with a thud rattling the glasses on the table.

Caesar watched his brother for a moment he could tell Armand was troubled.

"I know. Father told me, and although I am touched; I must admit a part of me wouldn't have done the same for you. Would I like to be alpha? Of course, what wolf worth his weight wouldn't? But that is not our way and just know when you take over you will have my and Evelyn's full support. I will not challenge your rule."

Armand met his eyes he didn't take offense to the revelation; his brother was very much like their father. Ambition flowed through his veins; he was an idealist. The young wolf craved absolute power or nothing at all.

Before he could respond the waiter returned and quickly took their order. He disappeared but kept a watchful eye on the two from afar.

They ate lunch, Caesar ever the timekeeper wanted to return to the office to finish up their quarterly meeting.

The drive back was silent with Armand forgetting the conversation at the restaurant choosing to focus on his return home party.

Caesar stole glances at his brother noting the distant stare.

"You know brother, I could set up a couple of 'accidental' run ins."

Armand thought it over. Would it be so bad to meet with her alone? He figured after two meetings he could have his appetite sated and then forget her.

"Sure, but I want to be included on everything."

Caesar was shocked at the response and nearly rear ended a silver Hyundai that had made a sudden stop. The two lurched forward before falling against the leather seats.

"I wasn't expecting that; are you sure?" Caesar asked as the car began to move again.

"Me either and yes." Armand stated as Caesar sped through a yellow light.

Another block and Caesar was whipping into his personal space in the parking garage. He opened the door hoping out of the car before leaning down, "leave everything to me." He slammed the door hurrying toward the elevator.

Armand let out a low groan this is what he was afraid of.

AMELIA FELT EYES ON her as she walked and oddly it filled her with excitement. She didn't know why or how but she could sense that he, Armand, was watching. She knew the building she passed earlier was the main offices for DuBois Enterprise and since he was back more than likely he was there.

She attempted to steal a glance upwards toward to the large windows of the building but was hurried along by the girls before she could focus her gaze. Due to her absentmindedness, the group almost got caught in the intersection.

The young heir was becoming an ever-increasing thought since the gala; he was becoming harder to shake and even her libido had awakened. She attempted to please herself as her best friend suggested but it felt cheesy and silly with the low-rate porno in the background.

She had barely touched herself before opting to stop and wait for the real thing.

Uncharacteristically, a part of her wanted the real thing to be with Armand. Thoughts of him were interrupted by tugging on her left arm, it was Ava the youngest of the group. The fifteen-year-old gifted Hispanic girl was her favorite although she never displayed it. As the girls pulled her into the small café thoughts of Armand were put on hold.

An Old Foe and New Friends

Gathering information on Armand had proven more difficult than Camille initially anticipated. He had no friends. No known associates. After several lunch dates and a boring dinner with a very forward ex-council member, Camille had a name. Cain Lewis.

The two had gone to Dartmouth together and were inseparable. Cain, the chubby rich kid of a prominent family, was always Armand's permeant plus one during the first two years of the boys' college days.

It had taken her nearly three weeks to track the man down. After several phone calls and emails to the ivy league school she got a lead that led her to a friend of a friend that once worked for the man in question.

She arrived at the call box and pressed the white button.

"Can I help you?" a foreign woman's voice came over the speaker.

"Camille, for Cain Lewis." There was a brief silence and Camille began to think he had changed his mind.

She settled back into the driver's seat and was about to reverse when the iron gate began to open, and Camille drove the Ashton Martin up to the main house.

She got out of the car and took a moment to take in the beach over the cliff and the floor to ceiling glass walls of the house. It was impressive and the real estate agent in her couldn't help but estimate the price at about eight million, but she still scoffed.

The mansion was gaudy and screamed playboy bachelor pad a cliché that had become a rite of passage for new money and an idea that the established old money bought into. Her attention was directed to a man coming toward her. He had on a pair of shades, and she could instantly sense that he was wolf as well.

"Ms. Knight?"

"Yes."

"Follow me please. Mr. Lewis is waiting for you."

She followed unaware she was being watched from the second floor.

When she initially called he had been wary about accepting the meeting wondering if it was a set up by Hemesh to ensure he had kept his end of the bargain.

Absentmindedly, he traced his index finger down the scar that ran across his face another gift from his once close friend. All these years he dreamed of paying Armand back.

Camille was led to a small first floor office.

"Mr. Cain will be with you shortly."

Cain entered about a minute later and Camille took in his physique. He was tall, well-built and reminded her a lot of Armand. She looked away trying to find the hatred she had earlier for the man that had used her over the years for a quick lay and then discarded her.

He approached his hand outstretched. She took it. Cain gave it a firm but friendly squeeze before releasing it and directing her to the chairs at the front of the desk.

"Thank you for meeting with me." Camille sat and crossed her leg as she placed her clutch on the frosted glass.

Cain sat in the chair next to her. He sat staring at her before quirking an eyebrow.

"Why are you here?"

Camille looked down briefly before she locked eyes with him smiling, "I thought I was clear on the phone why I was here."

"You gave what I thought was a bullshit reason. You're not here from the Dartmouth Historian Society. I looked it up doesn't exist and from one phone call I know that you are Armand's fuck buddy. Or well used to be if you are here trying to dig up dirt. So, Camille, why are you here? Did Hemesh or Max send you?"

Camille wore a sly smile on her full lips as she watched him cocking her head to the side like a small schoolgirl before running her eyes over the long scar across his face.

"How did you get the scar?"

Cain laughed, "you have no right to come in my home and start questioning me. I'll ask again and I expect an answer, or you can get the hell out. Now, why are you here?"

She pursed her lips before deciding to drop the act.

"I am looking for information."

Cain ran his eyes over the long legged blonde and leaned forward slightly.

"What type of information?"

"Hmm, let's say something a future alpha, the eldest son of a well-known family would find let's say embarrassing or what's the word I am looking for detrimental to his authority if it were to get out. We can't have someone with a tainted past heading our coven now can we?"

Cain sat back wanting to know more. It was merely out of curiosity he didn't need any prodding to go after Armand or his father, but he did need a proxy and if the gorgeous woman in front of him was willing then he would provide whatever she needed.

"Let's just say that I may have something that would do a lot of damage to the golden boy if it were to get out, but what's in it for me?"

Camille uncrossed her legs and slid closer on bottom barely on the edge of the chair, "revenge."

Cain smirked, "what makes you think I want revenge?"

"Hmm, just a hunch. You see Cain just like you I did some research before I called. You and Armand were old buddies always by each other's side a real bromance. Then you got that scar and Armand got transferred across the Atlantic to Oxford. You were left to deal with his mess. What did his Mommy say something?"

Cain's leg began to bounce as he thought back to the last semester of their sophomore year. Danielle had been around, so Cain decided to woo her, but Armand was against him seducing a human.

Cain soon learned it wasn't because his friend was concerned for his well-being or their true identify being discovered; it was because Armand desired the young virgin for himself.

The details were foggy, but for Cain everything was clear. He woke that morning to find the room covered in blood and the young woman lying on the floor a large portion of her throat missing.

The two sat in silence for several minutes Cain watching Camille. *Could she be trusted?* The question ran through his mind as he locked eyes with her, but he had a better question. *Could she be of use?*

For twelve years he had holed up in his beach side home seething and nursing his hatred. He was a pariah and reminiscing was the worst. What remained of his clan was scattered the name carried with it a smear that no amount of money could wipe away.

Solitude gave him lots of time much of which he spent researching and digging up information not only on Armand and the DuBois family but his own lineage. His late-night calls and meetings disguised as business trips to protect the last remaining witnesses of Maximillian's crimes revealed much that he had not known. His true birth right had been stolen from him.

He ground his teeth fighting back his anger. His time would come.

"How do I know if I can trust you? Who's to say that a few sweet words from the debonair Armand won't sway you away from our noble cause?"

She chuckled, "Armand is occupied with someone else, an Amelia Anaheim; she's the daughter of Max's good friend Charles. I thought it was some arrangement but apparently, he's into her."

"And you want revenge because he's no longer interested?"

"No, I want to teach him a lesson. Men like him always get their way with no consequences and people like me and you have to pick up the pieces in the aftermath. Besides someone needs to stop him. That whole family needs to be stopped not just Armand."

"So, you think we are the ones to do just that?"

He smiled it was nearly as gruesome as the scar he wore the pulled skin giving him a nefarious look.

"Why not? Who else has the balls to take down Prince Armand?" She asked spitting out the name.

Cain took a lingering sip from his glass.

He smiled nodding, "I think we have a deal. How about we talk more in depth over dinner?"

Camille smiled giving him a shy nod. He leaned forward and pressed a button on a small intercom within seconds a voice appeared on the other end.

"Yes, Mr. Lewis?"

"Set the table for two, I have a guest."

"Right away Mr. Lewis."

He stood looking down at Camille his hand extended, "shall we? It appears we have much to discuss."

Camille took his hand slowly rising her face a few inches from his given any other circumstance it would almost appear romantic.

"Yes we do, Mr. Lewis."

"Cain. Call me Cain."

The food was decadent, and Camille had eaten more than she normally did. She always kept an eye on her model figure but tonight she didn't mind, nor did she want to offend her host. He would play an integral part in her take down of Armand, so she needed him to view her favorably.

With the last of the silverware cleared following the last course, Cain leaned forward.

"What else do you want to know."

CAMILLE LEFT NEARLY five hours later. She hadn't planned on staying long but when Cain learned more of her background, they figured they could be more effective joined together. Unlike her, Cain was very familiar with Armand's past and the dead girl Danielle.

But a part of her was a little afraid, this was Armand and Maximillian they were going up against. Armand's father was a founding member of the Coven and Camille wouldn't doubt his sister, brother and mother would join in the group effort to protect their family and monetary livelihood at all costs.

The blonde wasn't under any illusions. Cain's agreement to this plan was more of a need, and what he needed was a cover someone that he could work through without getting his hands dirty, but she was smart and now that she had a starting point, she could work her way backwards.

You don't hang with a person like Armand and keep your hands clean.

Now, she needed more on Cain just in case they were discovered before the endgame was achieved and decided a trip to her accomplice's old stomping ground was in order.

She sped around the curve her thumbs lightly stroking the steering wheel.

This was exhilarating and terrifying.

THE PAST.

"Why should I help you?" The woman was old, and Maximillian could sense it although her skin was firm and flawless the slighter of light from the afternoon sun causing her angular face to have an unnatural glow.

He pushed the check forward across the table the skin of his finger catching on a small piece of the splintered wood.

"Money," he followed by placing the folded letter next to the cashier's check, "and better accommodations for you and your little girl." He nodded toward the toddler lurking at the threshold to the kitchen.

She laughed it was throaty, rich, and yet had an eeriness that bothered him sending a chill up his spine causing the thin hairs on his arm to rise.

"What makes you think Gianna and I don't like it here?" She stopped laughing and gestured around the room, "many would kill for such grand accommodations." Her voice dripped with sarcasm, and he sat up straighter pulling his blazer tighter in an attempt to disguise his shaking frame. It was the middle of summer but here deep in the woods it was unnaturally chilly.

Maximillian looked around trying his best not to sneer at the rough floorboards and the lack of basic amenities. The cabin was rugged giving the feeling he was out west during the pioneer days.

"Well, I to have a small child," once again he looked over at the girl just as she peeked around the door frame her large eyes a dark lavender wide with innocence and yet they were full of knowledge. He quickly thought of his son Armand and how all of this would be for him. He once again fought against the sneer that was attempting to form on his lips. What he needed to aid him he couldn't get anywhere else nor did he or anyone in his sphere knew how to make such a concoction.

"You possible can't like it here a child has many needs."

She raised her hand, "me nor Gianna, that's her name Maximillian," she hissed spittle forming at the corners of her mouth, "wouldn't be here if you and the likes of you accepted us." She leaned back in her seat.

He sighed; she was referring to the decree's exclusion of half-breeds. That weren't recognized many of them bastards; the only proof they had contact with humans outside of the necessary business deals needed to fund their livelihoods.

"Well once I am alpha things will change. A new dawn so to speak will take place," he stated looking down at the rough wood.

She hissed, "you want to kill this man?"

Maximilian's head snapped up his dusty denim blue irises locking with the woman's rum-colored ones. His mind quickly went to the two glasses he drank before he and Charles made the drive. His friend had agreed to wait in the car ever the coward he wanted to reap the benefits if he came out successful but wanted to keep enough distance in case he wasn't. The man was all about plausible deniability.

Nikki laughed again this time it vibrated off the bare walls and died before the sound made it back to his ears.

"If you are to carry this out, you need to become better at your poker face," she pointed at him, "if your desire is to become alpha you need to become a tactician a politician of considerable gift. I can assist with all but..." she leaned forward, "what's in it for me?"

"Recognition, wealth, access everything that you have been denied due to your...blood status. As a descendent of the Spencers you would have the full benefits placed upon you and your daughter."

She breath deep intrigued by the idea of gaining the recognition denied to her by her paternal side of the family. Her mother, a human, died in childbirth and Nikki was given to an aunt to raise. The woman was kind always reminding her of her true nature and all that she was due. That same aunt schooled her in the ways of the woods and most importantly the art of witchcraft.

"Hmm, I accept. What is it that you want?"

"You're right, I want someone dead. He's powerful, stronger than I am, and he has someone that I love very dearly."

"Ahh, so your motivated by love? Or Power? Which of these forces drives you toward this choice?"

He shook his head, "both. A young woman I love more than anything is in his crosshairs. She was promised to him, and they are set to marry soon. He's suffocating us. Destroying the Coven and everything I helped build from within. He's becoming more ruthless; he won't stop unless something is done to stop him."

"You believe you are the one?"

"Yes, I should have been the one to lead in the beginning but..." he trailed off too ashamed to admit he had been afraid of Samuel and the raw power he held. It was unnatural. He held power that couldn't be explained by his wolf heritage alone.

"You were scared, you don't have to explain. Who is this person? Another wolf I assume."

"Yes, as for the identity of this person that is irrelevant. Can you help me or not? I need something that can weaken him. Do you have it or not?" Maximilian was starting to become annoyed and angry.

Madame Nikki sensed she had stalled long enough and stood slowly her eyes never once leaving those of her guest.

Slowly she turned and disappeared over the threshold. The young girl briefly stepping to the side before she entered the kitchen to came to stand next to Maximillian.

"Hi." She whispered dirty blonde curly locks obscuring most of her round pudgy face.

"Hi." He whispered back his eyes watery. The young man felt he was running of time and losing everything. The wedding of Samira and Samuel was due to take place next month giving him less than three weeks to make everything right.

The woman emerged and in one quick motion grabbed the little girl by the arm and guided her out the room. Nikki returned a sly smile on her face as she sat.

She held up the small vial. The liquid reminded him of something gelatinous and he curled up his nose in disgust imaging that the substance would taste as horrendous as it looked.

"Ah, no this isn't a poison to drink. It's to be injected." She tapped the glass with a long nail. It was as if she had read his thoughts and Max involuntarily shuddered.

"How am I supposed to get that in his veins? I'm not a damned doctor!" He shouted feeling the trip had been a waste of time.

"No, you aren't but your friend, Charles, parked down by the lake is and from what I hear a damn good one." She raised an eyebrow, and he sat back in the chair staring at her his mouth slightly agape.

"But I...he's afraid. He won't get involved."

"Yes, he is reluctant but offer him something. What does he want most? Talk to him and you will find the two of you want the same outcome, to see this Samuel dead." She handed him the vial, "find out his desire and you shall have your accomplice."

Maximillian left clutching the vial close to his chest. Briefly, a slither of something akin to guilt ran through him but it was quickly replaced with relief. Samira would be free of Samuel, and so would he and they could be together.

He would take his place as alpha a leader that could bring them onto the world stage as a coven of American wolves that could stand proud next to the more established and wealthier ones.

He opened the passenger door sliding silently onto the warm leather.

Charles stared at the man a moment waiting for him to speak.

Maximillian remained silent as Charles started the motor of the Benz and slowly backed away from the still dark water.

Once they were on the gravel rode Charles decided to speak.

"So, what happened? Did you get what you needed?"

Maximillian was still quiet.

Charles snapped his fingers and waved his hand in front of the passenger's face frantically.

"Max, please, was she of any help? Did she give you anything?"

Maximillian slowly trailed his gaze away from the dashboard and to his friend that unbeknownst to the slightly younger man had guided the car to the side of the road.

"Yeah, she did," slowly he opened his hand revealing the small glass vial.

Charles snatched the vial holding it up in front of his face to get a better view.

"*What the hell is this shit?*" *He was sweaty and nervous.*

He shook the vial and snarled when the contents only moved slightly before it clung to the sides becoming immobile the harder he shook. Charles casually threw the vial back to him causing it to fall into Max's lap before rolling to the floor of the car.

"*Damn Charles, what the fuck? Our lives hinge on this,*" *he managed to get out as he folded his bulky frame at an odd angle snatching the object from the floor.*

"*You gave that old hag a hundred grand for this shit,*" *he stated pointing at the contents as Maximillian placed it inside his pocket.*

"*Yes, I wanted to make sure we gave her enough, she has a little girl living in that dump.*"

Charles hissed as he guided the car back to the center of the rode, "*don't start getting all sentimental on me now. You are the one that wants the man dead. I can deal with Samuel; I mean give him what he wants and stay out of his way. Things are pretty good the money is rolling in.*" *He looked over at his friend.*

"*Yes, and deep down you want him dead as well. He's not good for anyone.*"

"*You mean he's not good for Samira.*"

Maximillian's eyes went wide, and he bristled.

"*Don't bring her up.*"

Charles sighed, "*you're married with a son. You need to let this cub love you two have go. She's engaged to Samuel she's going to be his wife. What about that don't you get?*"

The driver through up his free hand.

"*It's not that simple,*" *the breath he released was strained and he tried to sink into the leather. He always felt small when his wife and son were brought up and a feeling of betrayal followed.*

"*Yeah, it is, Max. She's off limits. What is it about her? I mean you haven't had sex with the woman in what two years or so.*" *He stated chuckling until his eyes fell on those of Maximillian.*

He quickly stopped, "oh God, don't tell me you're still fucking her!" Charles shouted as he stomped on the brakes, the car fish tailed kicking up gravel as it came to a stop lurching the two occupants forward.

"Dammit Charles you're going to fucking kill us!"

"You damned impulsive lovesick idiot. We are dead anyway if this gets out that you have been sleeping with his fiancée. Are you thinking at all?"

"Yes Charlie, yes I am thinking I may be lovesick, but I am not a greedy money grubbing son of bitch like you!"

"Fuck you, my money grubbing is the reason you can give that old bitch a hundred grand." He turned in his seat his finger inches away from Maximillian's face.

"Do you know what I had to do to hide that money?"

"Please Charles that watch you bought Diane costed just as much if not more." He through his hand up shifting his body away from Charles.

"No, since you have been tucked away in your love cocoon changes have been made."

Maximillian stared at his friend, "what changes? What does his majesty require now?"

"All transactions have to be justified with the high table and therefore Samuel both personal and business related."

"What! Bullshit! You see he wants absolute control absolute power. This," he pulled the poison from his pocket, "will change all of that."

Charles shook his head, "what is that shit anyway? Besides how are we going to get him to drink that shit, what pour it in morning bourbon?" He sighed gripping the stirring wheel.

"No," he paused placing the vial back in his pocket fearing that what he said next would send the man over the edge, "it has to go in intravenously; that's where you come in."

Lighting fast Charles through the car in drive and floored the gas pushing them into the crushed leather.

"You have a fucking death wish?" They quickly picked up speed and in a vain attempt Maximillian gripped the side bar overhead.

A thought of reaching for the steering wheel crossed his mind but he feared they would wreck on the rural road, and this deep in the backwoods they would not be found.

"No, slow down you're going to get us killed!"

They skid to a stop kicking up gravel that bounced off the Benz's bumper. He through the car in park and turned to Maximillian.

"No, you are going to get all of us killed! This goes beyond going behind his back we are talking about killing a man with poison."

"No, Charlie we are talking about weakening a man so that we can challenge. He is too strong to go the traditional route besides with the exception of you and me everyone is his friend or a relative. Doesn't exactly make things impartial does it."

"No, so you can challenge."

"When I win you too will reap the benefits of this."

"If you win then we will reap the benefits mostly you. Remember you become alpha and I...what remain a council member with no upward mobility. I would be trading one tyrant for another."

"That's not it. I am offering true partnership; I don't want to rule over anybody Charles besides you have ideas and hopes for this just like we all did in the beginning before he involved himself."

Charles sighed falling back into his seat. He needed a moment to think. He like several others were not happy with the style of leadership nor the person in charge. The man was a bully laying claim to whatever he felt entitled.

As the Coven's main doctor many of the elite members came to him for medical treatment and so did Samuel. He had access question remained did he have the heart to do it.

He closed his eyes.

"He has a medical exam coming up," he hesitated, "I can do it then."

Maximillian could tell his friend was struggling. He reached out and placed his hand on the man's shoulder. Charles shook it off but turned to face him once again.

"*Can or will, Charlie?*"

"*I will do it; is that what you need to hear, but there is something I want as well. My daughter and your son Armand. I want them betrothed and when they come of age I want them married.*"

Charles lips were now a thin line and his eyes hard the trepidation from before was gone. Max saw the change in mood as the first step it meant that his friend was ready to bargain. He just needed to take Madame Nikki's advance and figure out what more did his friend of more than twenty years want.

"*So, you want me to force my son to marry your daughter? Is that it?*"

Charles chuckled shaking the steering wheel.

"*Of course not. I want to head the Table of Selene. I want the chairman's seat.*"

Maximillian thought for a moment.

"*But you head the council.*"

"*For what I am doing for you, you are lucky I am not asking to for more. Like your first-born daughter.*"

"*You reach too far my friend.*" *Max was resigned he didn't want to agree. Before his son was born he and Hemesh had agreed on one thing, they would not put their children into an arranged marriage. Although they had found a middle ground, many days had been difficult with the two of them avoiding one another. He didn't want his children to suffer the same fate.*

"*Well, I learned from the best. So,*" *he extended his hand,* "*we have a deal? I inject whatever that crap is into his veins and when the time comes you deliver the final blow.*"

Max nodded reaching for the outstretched hand. Charles took it squeezing it hard. Max looked from their conjoined hands to the other man's face. It was hard once again, and his eyes had taken on a darker hue causing his almond-colored eyes to shift to a coffee black.

"*Once we go down this road there is no turning back. You must kill him. No getting cold feet on this one Max.*"

Maximillian returned the force by squeezing slightly.

"I know. I will kill him and as for your daughter and my son consider it done. We are family now."

"You better and yes we are truly family now." He nodded releasing his hand. Charles fired up the Benz and the two continued down the rural road.

Hypothetical

The young CEO had rifled through paperwork the majority of the morning. He expected some dirt but nothing of this magnitude. His brother was a murderer and in DuBois fashion his father and mother had covered it up.

He only wanted to gather information about the Coven to start a historical society to give more legitimacy to the American branch. Since the engagement to his African fiancée, he wanted to use the bridging of covens and cultures to launch his plans for the alliance of wolves around the world.

But a simple search and inquiry into their history led him down a rabbit hole for which he couldn't climb out of. His meeting with some of the older members gave him names and often led to many literal dead ends. He soon found out that all were associated with his father and the Coven's origins.

Many of the people he found were residents of the cemetery some had disappeared entirely leaving only confused and scared family members behind. Some were forth coming others were not. He quickly learned during his interviews not to reveal that he was a DuBois. He had one elderly man attack him with a broom. He had entered the man's mobile home and was offered coffee until he introduced himself this time stating his last name. The old man bristled dropping the ceramic cup as he moved with a swiftness Caesar hadn't expected in a hundred and ten year old wolf.

Unfortunately, the near misses and fear continued the further he dug causing him to give an alias.

Sarah, a middle-aged woman, and the grand-daughter of a Martha Wiltshire had grown fearful and nearly broke down in tears when he revealed his identity. She thought he had come to kill her.

Aside from the name Wiltshire repeatedly appearing alongside his father's another name appeared Charles William Anaheim, a longtime friend of his father and one of the founding families and the head of their governing body.

The deaths and the missing documents all were the result or related to the origin of the Coven.

There were missing pieces still, but Caesar had enough to draw conclusion as he compared his notes. One person he could not find no matter how hard he or his minions searched was a Wiccan woman and half wolf that went by the name – Madame Nikki.

He stood in front of the dilapidated cabin it was held in trust by DuBois Enterprise. At first, he was curious after his dive into Madam Nikki this address kept coming up. He wanted to know why their father would purchase such a place and leave it standing.

CAESAR DROVE UP TO the large manor and rang the doorbell. It wasn't polite for him to come calling without prior notice, but this was something he didn't want to discuss over the phone. A plan formed, and after discussing all he had found over the last few months with Evelyn and with the return of his brother, he had the confidence to move forward.

A small woman opened the door eyeing him with her left eye. The other was was a milky white and Caesar speculated she from the older generation of wolves, he guessed the woman was nearly a hundred.

"It's impolite to call at this hour."

The young wolf stole a glance at his watch, "well, I understand it's early, but I have a pressing matter that I need to discuss with the mistress of the house. May I come in?"

The old woman whispered in a foreign language before she mumbled a harsh "wait" slamming the door in his face.

He stood rocking on the balls of his feet impatient before he heard more of the foreign language this time the voice was clear half a century younger.

The door opened and he was met with Diane's smiling face.

"Mr. DuBois what brings you here? Please come in," she stepped to the side. He entered leaning down to place a chaste kiss on her cheek.

He looked around, "is your husband available? If possible, I would like to speak to you both." Caesar through in wanting to include Charles, but really, he already knew the man had left for the morning. He watched him depart from the backseat of the town car.

Diane looked confused before answering, "no, he's left for the office."

"Can we speak somewhere more private it's regarding my brother and Amelia." He raised his eyebrow and Diane took the hint.

"Aunt Nancy, get breakfast started. I have business to discuss with Mr. DuBois see that we are not disturbed."

Diane turned her attention back to Caesar, "follow me." He trailed her into the first floor library.

She closed the door behind them, and Caesar sat on the small sofa Diane joined him pulling her robe sash a little tighter out of nervousness.

"I suppose you can guess why I'm here." Caesar began waiting for Diane to respond.

"I make no assumptions Mr. DuBois."

"Please Caesar, after all if things progress smoothly, I suppose we'll be family by next spring."

Diane smiled liking what she was hearing.

"Go on Caesar."

"My brother has expressed interest in Amelia not just from the party last week but he has a continued interest which we both know is rare."

Diane looked at her nails doing her best to show disinterest. She didn't want to appear too eager.

"A man's interest is fleeting Caesar especially where your brother is concerned."

Diane needed some type of confirmation that Armand had a genuine interest. Although whether he had one or not her daughter and the eldest DuBois wouldn't have a say given her husband's stance on the issue.

"See, that's how I know Armand has an interest he's even asked me to arrange some chance," he drew the word out looking at Diane keenly, "encounters. That's where you come in Mrs. Anaheim."

She smirked, "I need more than 'chance encounters' my daughter is more than a weekend fling."

"I understand a great deal is at stake here. My brother is set to be the future alpha take over the Coven, it's financials, the works. Just think of all the influence your family would have."

"I think you are forgetting Caesar; I am married to one of the founding members of the Coven. I already have influence."

"Yes, but limited power. Although a member of one of the founding families, you nor any of your bloodline can rise to alpha but think a moment. Once my brother takes the mantle and with Amelia by his side by marriage and through your daughter let's say one of your sons could challenge or rather Mr. Anaheim."

He flicked a piece of imaginary lint off his forearm as he leaned back into the sofa.

Diane's smirk faded, "what you speak of is treason."

"Is it? The DuBois or rather my father has a very lose definition of treason. I think this is something your husband knows all too well. Besides, we are just talking this is a simple exercise in the hypothetical."

She sighed catching his meaning. For one of her sons to become alpha was one thing but imagine if her husband could take the mantle Diane could imagine a near infinite number of possibilities.

"Let's keep with this hypothetical exercise as you say, where would this leave Amelia? I won't turn her out into the cold simply because her husband lost a challenge. Besides Caesar, you are the second son why would you want to remove the inheritance of alpha from your family? What do you gain by seeing an Anaheim at the helm?"

"Simple solution; once my brother has been challenged and loses Amelia will be returned back to the home of her father. As for me, my talents extend beyond just the position of head of a pack. You see Mrs. Anaheim, I am a king maker a facilitator if you will now what do I gain? I would say head of the council as a friendly gesture for the life of my brother."

Diane smiled believing she was seeing eye to eye with the young man.

"I understand."

The youngest DuBois male returned her smile his plan was starting to come into play. He just needed to gather the final players giving them the information they would need in order to accomplish what he couldn't on his own.

"Good."

"Please, call me Diane as you have stated we will be family by next spring." She crossed her legs.

"What did you have in mind for the first encounter?"

"DuBois Enterprise is having their mid-year charity gala. I was thinking it's a good a place as any. Plus, it shows the giving side of my brother." He smirked.

"I will make sure she is there; you rein in your brother and make sure his eyes are on her."

"I assure you that won't be a problem."

"Good."

Diane stood extending her hand.

Caesar rose as well taking the woman's hand and giving it a firm shake.

"I look forward to our partnership."

"Likewise, Diane. I'll send over several events, and we can collaborate accordingly," he stated his long lean form towering over hers.

"Let me see you out." She led him to the front door the two just like earlier exchanged chaste kisses and Caesar departed heading toward the office.

Invitation and Information

U*NKNOWN* flashed in bold letters across the screen. Out of habit, she didn't hesitate to let it go to voice mail. With a small sigh Camille slid further down into the tub basking in the balmy water.

It rang again; sitting up she let out a hiss and dried her hand. In a quick grabbing motion she snatched the phone from the small table next to the claw foot tub bringing it to her ear.

She sighed annoyed and her tone conveyed it, "hello?" The greeting came out harsh and dry.

"The DuBois Enterprise Charity Gala on September 3rd, very exclusive event. So exclusive in fact that I don't see your name on the list."

"Who is this?"

"Simply put a mutual friend, better question what are you going to wear? There's a box at your front door containing your invitation. I suggest you don't lose it, you will not receive a second one, and you will need it to enter."

"Who the hell is this? Is this a joke?"

"As I said before a mutual friend, and no Camille, I don't joke around."

"How do you know my name?" reflexively she looked at the threshold to the bathroom half expecting someone to enter.

A deep chuckle bounced around in her inner ear, "I'm not in your house. Besides, you should get out of the bath and get your package looks like it's about to rain."

"Who the fuck is this?" Camille was becoming angry.

"No need for hostilities, like I said earlier a friend, but you can consider me a facilitator if you will. We both share a common goal. You and I want to knock the golden boy off his pedestal."

She stood placing the robe around her body balancing the phone between her shoulder and ear. Temporarily, she removed the device sliding the silk over her shoulders.

Camille hurried downstairs and paused at the front door before she quickly jerked it opened peeking around the frame for the mystery caller.

"Most women regardless of being wolf would be cautious of opening their door with a stranger on the phone. Especially one that is watching." The voice on the other end taunted.

She picked up the package turning it over in her hand, "well I'm not most women human or wolf."

"Of course, not Camille. The invitation is also good for a plus one so bring your buddy Cain, I'm sure he would love to see his old friend again."

Before she could respond the line went dead. She looked at the cell before placing it in the pocket of her robe and stepping back inside hovering at the edge of the threshold. She couldn't see anything in the gated yard and quickly scanned the large hill in the background.

She couldn't distinguish any features but saw the outline of a figure in all black the face covered by a mask. She didn't see any binoculars, so Camille speculated the mysterious caller was wolf as well. Her suspicions were confirmed when the figure waved before disappearing beyond the tree line.

Camille slammed the door. She wouldn't waste time attempting to search for a scent trail if the person was smart which she assumed they were they would have covered those bases. Once again she looked around slightly unnerved as she went to the large window and pulled the drapes.

She went back upstairs and placed the invitation on the bed staring at the maroon envelope as she dressed in a cashmere lounge set. Once done she belly flopped next to it. If he knew about Cain that meant she was being followed and would need to discover the identity of this mystery person. A discovery she would rather uncover sooner than later.

The phone rang again this time she recognized the number as that of her contact she had hired to look into Cain.

"Do you have anything?"

"I wouldn't call if I didn't." The voice was raspy and carried an edge to it.

"Well?" Camille was growing annoyed.

"Easy there, I am at the gate."

She rolled her eyes, "really? You couldn't have just emailed or tell me what you found over the phone?"

"No, what I have needs to be told in person. A phone call would have not sufficed."

"Fine." She hung up tossing the phone next to the envelope and headed downstairs.

Camille watched standing in the door as the black Buick pulled up. She down turned her lips in disgust.

The SUV came to a halt in the stone driveway and the engine turned off with a slight groan.

The driver got out looking around before slamming the door and hitting the lock button on the key fob.

She approached Camille, "you know you don't have to look at my car that way. I had to drop the kids off at soccer."

Camille rolled her eyes at her half-sister.

Gianna was nearly a striking image of Camille although twenty years older and was a half breed. The product of a brief love affair in college between their mother and a male student. The woman had been stunned when Gianna showed up on her doorstep seven years ago, but it had been a happy surprise to know the woman was also in the private investigation game running her own small firm.

Camille hadn't been too interested in making family connections, but Gianna's profession meant she had a ready PI at her disposal and all it required of her was the occasional phone call and lunch meet up. She had even gone as far as to buy the kids something for Christmas.

The model brought her older sister in the sitting room and gestured for her to take a seat.

Gianna sat looking around, "I see you made some changes."

"I did. Would you like something to drink? To eat?"

"No, I won't stay long. Tell me, what do you know about the Coven's origins and a Samuel Wiltshire?"

Camille slowly lowered herself onto the other end of the large couch.

"I am not familiar with the name and as for the Coven's origins I am not sure what this has to do with digging up information on Cain?" She whispered; the young wolf had a strange feeling she was about to hear information that would change everything.

"Just a brief overview sis," she crossed her legs leaning into the pillows, "the Coven was founded by four clans. That being the Raos, the Anaheims, the Wiltshires, and of course the DuBois as a safe haven and support system for every full-bloodied wolf in the country. It was meant to bridge the gap between the well-oiled and very wealthy wolf covens of Europe, India, and some of the African countries. At its inception it was agreed this coven was to be headed by a Wiltshire for the duration of its existence."

"I didn't know that. Essentially, the Wiltshire's setup a monarchy. That's a lot of power for one family to have but as you know a DuBois heads the Coven so how do you explain that? If I am reading between the lines, I can only speculate it wasn't through legitimate means."

Gianna chuckled, "I see you're more than perky tits and pretty teeth."

The young woman rolled her eyes sighing. Her half-sister could be vulgar at times, but she attributed her language to her upbringing in the Alabama backwoods. She remained silent waiting for Gianna to continue.

"The original decree signed in blood states no member of the founding families nor anyone for that matter except a male member of the Wiltshire clan can lead, and get this, and only the those belonging to the Wiltshire clan can challenge. The reason a DuBois is currently at the helm is because of an amendment to the original decree naming the DuBois family as successors in the event there is no male Wiltshire after the alpha's death. It also gave the DuBois family the power to challenge."

Camille's lips parted slightly, "and the council agreed to this?"

"Initially, I had the same question as you, but it doesn't matter because Samuel agreed. However it's difficult for dead men to sign decrees. The answer would be yes especially when you have the head of the council advocating on your behalf. Some guy named Charles Anaheim. But the reason I bring this up is because your Cain Lewis is Cain Wiltshire."

For Camille the pieces were slowing falling into place.

"What happened to the former alpha?"

"Well, barely two years into his reign he becomes weak and less than three weeks later is challenged by Maximillian DuBois and killed. I have it on good authority the amendment was added after this Samuel was murdered."

"Murdered? Why do you say murdered? A challenge was issued, the man lost. Right?"

Gianna leaned to the side and picked up her bag off the floor. She pulled out a Manila envelope and handed it to Camille smirking.

"That right there is an independent autopsy report Cain had performed last year. There was enough poison in Samuel's body to drop two elephants but given that he was full wolf it weakened him significantly that's when I can only assume your boy Max went in for the kill."

"So, does Cain know this as well?" Camille looked up from the papers.

"I can only assume yes, if not he is quickly putting the pieces together. So, whatever you have with this Cain fellow I would end it. You are about to step into a full out war between two of the founding families; and I would stay clear of the DuBois. All of them. Especially, that Armand. He may be a pretty boy and all but back during his sophomore year he raped and ripped out a girl's throat. Allegedly of course there's no evidence; at least none I could find.

Camille leaned forward, this must have been what caused the rift between Cain and Armand.

"Did you get a name?"

"Yeah, Danielle Fields. She was from Vermont."

She fell back into the cushion stunned. "I don't think Armand would do something like that."

Her sister scoffed, "why? Because the two of you were fuck buddies at one point? Ah, don't give me that look, just because I cut you a discount doesn't mean I am not good at what I do. I know about your clandestine trips to Spain. That's a long way to go for a booty call." She chuckled before once again becoming serious.

"That whole family is a terror. Hera, that little sister of theirs may be quiet and pretty but she's no angel. One of the sorority girls thought she'd have a little fun at Hera's expense let's say the girl ended up in a coma for two weeks. That was over a year ago poor girl still won't talk about it. His little brother Caesar is downright foul. He just settled out of court for three and a half million for intimidation among other things. Not to mention, some guys wanted to play hardball and unionize. The lead man was found floating down the Black Warrior. Details of how he got there are foggy and hard to pin down. These are some very nasty characters. So you need to be careful." Gianna added.

"I can take care of myself." Camille said harsher than intended truth was she was terrified at what all this would mean if she wasn't successful. There was only one way this ended, and the outcome wasn't favorable.

"I don't think you get it. Or maybe jetting off to Paris with mom has left you out of touch. This isn't some wolf remake of *Gossip Girl* and you've stumbled on some hot dormitory tea about who's wearing last season's Prada. Samuel's sister thought it was strange her brother would hand over all that he spearheaded to a hothead like this Max fellow, so she did a little digging. She started asking questions you know making a little noise. Let's just say Martha's head and body ended up in separate rooms in her house. One of the maids found her. It's safe to say they don't handle threats well."

Camille thought for a moment, "can you get me more information on the DuBois and Wiltshires?"

Gianna stood, "you give great gifts, and you pay pretty decent but no. While I was diving into the very interesting history of the American Coven and meeting some very unsavory individuals I stumbled upon more disappearances and murders either sanctioned by that family directly or indirectly than I care to count. Anything more and you must find someone else. Maybe a few years ago before Amy and the boys but not now. I am not adding to their body count and if you are smart, which I think you are, you would do the same and leave this, whatever it is, alone."

She placed her bag on her shoulder, "I'll see myself out." Gianna headed toward the front door.

Camille watched the retreating lace clad back and deep tan shoulders of her sister. She needed to process all she heard. That meant Cain was using her to grind an axe with not only Armand but the DuBois clan as well. She went upstairs papers in hand.

She sat up long into the early morning debating whether she wanted to proceed with this course of action. Camille wasn't sure if she wanted to be caught in the middle of a war between Cain and Armand. Just before dawn she made her decision. For the time being, Camille would play along as she would need more time to wiggle her way out of her deal with the devil.

The Decree

T*he Past*
The sound of clinked glasses was drowned out by the laughter of the men. They had received the official word their coven would be recognized. Maximillian smiled as he thought of the long and formal letter penned on aged parchment that arrived that morning. The had the backing of all nine covens.

He watched as Samuel signed with two fluid strokes. Darsh and Charles followed both clinking glasses once they were done. Maximillian reluctantly picked up the pen and dipped it in the inkwell of blood. He hesitated above the parchment the smile he wore slowly evaporating.

This didn't sit well with him. He nor any of them for that matter had the right to challenge only male members of the Wiltshire clan. He sighed and was about to refuse when he felt a presence over his shoulder.

"Is there something wrong?"

It was Samuel his tone had an edge and the others sensing the tension stopped allowing silence to fill the room.

Max took a deep breath and turned to face the newly minted alpha.

"Something doesn't feel right Sam. Every pack member can challenge or at the very least has the right to do so. Even the Africans and they have some of the oldest covens in the world."

Samuel laughed, "yes and they are full of confusion and chaos. With our Rights of Challenge article this ensures there are no backdoor dealings or plots for power. Besides the council will serve as a check and balance to the alpha."

"It's only chaos in the lower nations. It's the tribes that won't modernize and..." Darsh trailed off squirming slightly under Samuel's intense gaze.

"As I was saying," he refocused on Maximillian, "chaos and confusion, everyone and anyone with a decent idea thinks he can lead. Some of them even let their women challenge. Imagine how quickly our newly formed coven would cease to exist without order. This decree will ensure the continuation for hundreds of years to come."

"With your bloodline?" Maximillian whispered catching looks of from Charles and Darsh. He stood up straighter doing his best to disguise his shaking hands.

"Yes, of course. Who else?" He stepped back turning to look at the other two men in the room. "Who else here is not only willing but worthy to take on the mantel as head of a coven? It is more than a notion gentleman the responsibility is great. The prosperity of nearly every wolf in the country, this continent even, will in someone way or another rely on the alpha. That is me. Seeing to the well-being of all is a cross that I will gladly bear."

He turned his attention back to Maximillian and approached the young man.

"Either Max, you are with me, with us, or you are against us. There can be no compromise, dissension will not be tolerated."

Samuel's cinnamon colored eyes shifted to a stone grey. Maximillian knew he wouldn't win but the young wolf wasn't so quick to back down from a fight.

Charles stepped forward placing a hand on each man's shoulder.

Samuel looked at Charles his gaze further intensifying. His stance was stiff and threatening; Charles felt the man's muscle tighten and he pulled back his hand quickly the other remained on Maximilian's shoulder.

"Max," Charles squeezed his friend's shoulder, "is simply worried that's all, but he sees the merit of your argument and is grateful that you and your great family have agreed to bear the burden of the coven's prosperity and continuation." He inclined his head in show of respect and submission.

Their self-appointed alpha's gaze remained intense, his body was wired, and he was on the verge of a full shift. Charles knew the next few words from either of them were crucial. Even a miscommunication on his part could cost him his life as well as that of his young friend.

Charles edged closer to Maximillian his grip becoming like a vice. His grin had grown tighter as he sought out eye contact to plead with him to stand down.

Seconds seemed like an eternity as Max averted his gaze and relaxed. For now, he would have to go along with the plan and sign the decree. There was no way he would win in a challenge. Even showing early signs of the change would be justification enough for Samuel to kill him just to set an example for the others.

He nodded and Charles let go releasing a breath he hadn't known he'd been holding.

The tall robust man nodded as well acknowledging the others submission. Samuel's expression smug as his muscles visibly uncoiled beneath his suit. Maximillian signed adding an extra flourish for appearance's sake, but he vowed to find a way to get rid of him.

They drank long into the night laying out the rules and foundations of this newly formed thing. Only Samuel did the talking with Charles and Darsh nodding in silent agreement. Max stood to the side of the three sipping at the glass of whiskey.

"Similar to the Europeans, all their assets are controlled by one family with oversight from a select and trusted few. Now our wealth isn't as large as theirs at least not yet, but I can oversee assets, invest them, and make sure they are protected." Darsh stated his eyes squinted as he ran the numbers in his head.

The tall thin Indian man continued, "I would say in three years we could be looking at around seven hundred million, in..."

He was cut off by Samuel, "no, as alpha, the remaining members of the Wiltshire clan and I will oversee all Coven assets."

Darsh nodded reluctantly.

"Okay, that's great, Max, Charles and I can provide the oversight." Darsh stated attempting to mask the unease he felt at basically establishing a monarchy.

Samuel eyeballed him and Darsh continued not picking up the que to be quiet, "just like the clans in England, they have a separate council that helps. Maybe we could implement..." Darsh trailed off as Samuel's gaze hardened. He knew it was wise not to continue.

Samuel spoke his gaze fixated on Darsh, "No oversight is needed; I assure you gentlemen your livelihoods are safe with me. No, in order for us to establish our dominance and compete with the other covens we must set our own ways and laws. Not become copies of the others."

His focused shifted to Maximillian. "You agree, Max?"

For the second time that evening, the room went silent Charles and Darsh exchanged worried glances hoping there wouldn't be a repeat of earlier. Neither was sure if Samuel would overlook a perceived second transgression.

"Yes?" he asked.

"Do you agree?" Samuel asked as he stood up straight. Charles noticed the slight twitch of the man's hand and took a small step behind Samuel so he could have a clear view of Maximillian.

Charles stared at his friend.

Maximillian approached them slowly and with his free hand fingered the papers near the end of the table.

"I agree. We are new therefore our ways won't be like the others," he locked eyes with the broad shoulder man, "I trust you and your great family. You have the oldest bloodline amongst us."

Samuel sighed placing his arm around Maximillian, "that's all I wanted Brother was your support. Let's put what happened before behind us."

He smiled pulling the shorter blond closer.

Maximillian smiled nodding, "of course Brother."

Darsh unclenched his fists and Charles clapped his hands together more to dissolve his own nervousness than excitement. He knew that agreeing to allow all they had funnel through the Wiltshire owned and operated bank would only make the Wiltshire's richer and more powerful but by mere osmosis they too would share in the wealth."

"It allows us enough time to consolidate our own lines of banking and strengthen our businesses. I agree." Darsh added nodding at Samuel and Maximillian.

Without any oversight, he would have to trust that Samuel and his family knew what they were doing when it came to growing the American coven's wealth. Without the money they had no hope of being taken seriously.

The talks and brandy only lasted another hour before the men drifted out. Darsh was the first to leave citing needing to return to his wife and their newborn son. Samuel soon followed still high from his power trip he decided he would pay the girls at Christie's a visit.

Charles lingered in the corner sitting in the recliner. His glass still full from earlier. He waited thirty minutes before he spoke; paranoia was getting the better of him and he was fearfully that Samuel had waited around to ease drop.

He stood and moved closer to his friend.

"Max," he spoke his name softly and waited.

Maximillian looked up at him his face neutral.

"I would advise you not to do that."

"Do what, Charlie?"

"Challenge him."

"If you noticed I didn't issue a challenge, not that I could due to that bullshit we just signed," he jumped up from his chair, "and what was that earlier? I thought you would have backed me up!" he shouted.

The slender dark brown skinned man remained calm watching as his friend paced back and forth before stopping his focus now on him;

Maximillian was angry he was too, but he would never express it so openly.

"And what Max? Get both of us killed, you and I have wives and our firstborns we must consider. Your Armand is barely one and my Amelia is only a few months old. Do you want them growing up without us? Only knowing what they have been told. And you know that he would paint us as the villains tarnish our names. They would throw Hemesh and Diane out on the streets! Is that what you want? You'd risk them to make a point!"

He raised his voice he was near shouting but reigned in his emotions when he saw his friend's shoulders drop.

"I am sorry. I just. We have talked about this for what three years, we did the work all for him to come in and set up a perpetual reign for his kin. It angered me Charlie and I shouldn't have let it get to me but..."

He sighed running his hands over his face, "he has to be stopped." He pointed at the door, "you see what he's doing? He's using our money, and our influence to build a fortress around himself. If he gets his way he will be unstoppable."

He turned in a circle and threw his hands in the air.

"Although I agree with you Max, there is nothing we can do. Not now besides what do we do?" He looked down at the floor, he wasn't excited at helping usher in the rein of the Wiltshires but there weren't any options. He had to accept the outcome and pray he could bear the burden of what they had allowed to happen.

"We get rid of him."

Charles rolled his eyes, "you know we can't win in a challenge Max tonight proved that. Neither one of us is strong enough to take him on."

"No, there are other means to weaken him. You're a doctor surely you know a thing or two."

Charles held up his hand, "no. Murder is not the answer either."

"There are ways, Brother..."

Charles cut him off, "I will not hear any of this; I am leaving before you say something that we both will regret."

"We can do it. I need your help."

Charles sighed, "it's too soon to stage a coup Max. Wait and bide your time. An arrogant ass like him is bound to slip up and you'll be there to show everyone the right path." He clasped his forearm, "but for now leave it alone don't feed into this madness."

He released him, "go home to your wife and son. Okay."

Charles turned and headed for the door. He grabbed his coat and put it on. As he placed his hand on the doorknob he turned slightly and through over his shoulder, "I understand Max, I want him dead too." With that statement he opened the door and quickly headed into the darkness leaving Maximillian alone.

MONTHS PASSED UNDER Samuel's dictatorship slowly. The man would not listen to reason and dealt harshly with dissenters. He secretly met with Darsh, the Indian man was in agreement with Maximillian and would offer his support only behind the scenes. Like the other six men that comprised the council he was afraid.

"Max, I want you to know I have only entertained this meeting because you are a friend, and we have a history. You very well know Samuel is set to marry my younger sister," he stared at strawberry blond hard, "I know about you and Samira. End it; she has been promised to him."

"More like he came in like a barbarian and declared her his bride."

"He's the alpha, we are under his dominion. I don't want you to get hurt nor my sisters, especially the one you're married to, Hemesh. Forget about her? What will happen to her if you are found to be conspiring against him?"

"He is leading us down a dangerous path. He is impulsive, throwing his weight around severing connections and pissing off members of other covens! Were you not there when he insulted the delegation from Chad? It was embarrassing."

Maximillian banged on the table with his closed fist, "we'll be lucky to get another meeting with them."

Darsh sighed rubbing sweat from his forehead. The two sat in a brief and uncomfortable silence.

"So, to make lemonade you...have to squeeze a few lemons."

"Not when those lemons are hanging from one of the most influential trees on the African continent. It will take years if not a decade or two to fix what his has done."

"Well," Darsh paused unsure of how to proceed he agreed with Maximillian.. He didn't agree with Samuel's form of dictatorship nor the marriage that was set to take place next spring between the man and his other sister.

"I'll give you this Max. In a few weeks, he will be my brother-in-law."

Max was about to protest until Darsh held up his hand.

"Let me finish, I don't agree with his ways, his leadership nor the marriage, but I have to comply." He hesitated, "given the circumstances in which my father has placed us all."

"Has there been threats?" Maximillian leaned forward.

"Not in so many words, if you have any love for my sister, you'd leave her be. Focus on Hemesh and the son she has borne you."

Maximillian looked away unable to bear Darsh's intense gaze. He had love for his wife always would, but it was nothing compared to the burning fire and desire he had for Samira.

"Hemesh is a great woman I will always care for her she's the mother of my heir, but I love Samira. She's my first choice always has been."

Darsh sighed he saw the man was genuine and although he came here partly to talk his friend out of pursuing his little sister he wouldn't address the matter any further. Their alpha and his antics were a more pressing concern.

"Regardless of the situation something has to be done about him. He's going to destroy us from the inside."

"Like what? We already sighed the decree, and we agreed to his authority not to mention recognizing the right of rule of his male lineage." Darsh whispered.

Fear governed his thoughts as well as paranoia. The mere fact they were meeting in secret was by Samuel's definition treason in of itself. If word got back to any of the other council members or Samuel for that matter, they were as good as dead.

"We didn't have much of a choice. There was no vote on anything we discussed and agreed to as a collective was put into the decree. Samuel wrote it..."

"And we went along with it. You forget Brother." Darsh added.

Darsh stood buttoning his blazer, "a bit of advice going forward, don't speak to anyone else about this. Many on the Council and the Table of Selene are growing very wealthy with Samuel's underhand and back alley deals. His spies all around. Oh, and this thing with Samira will cease, or I will go to Samuel myself. I won't have you making a fool out of my sister and a whore out of the other."

Before Maximillian could respond Darsh had stepped away from the table and was exiting the door of the private dining room.

He fell back in the chair, he thought if anyone would see reason it would have been Darsh, the pragmatic logical member of their little group. The senior council member waved over the waiter and, after paying the check, left.

He would have to focus on Charles and convince him of his cause, and he would have to move fast before his love was given away to the man he despised more than any other.

A Gala and a Memory

Camille lingered in the back, waiting for the DuBois brothers to make their entrance. The jaded young woman figured it would be the usual. The younger male of the alpha arrogantly gliding down the staircase fiancée on his arm. Except this time the pair would be joined by Armand. She sneered at the thought of him.

A waiter stopped in front of her, offering a tray of glasses surrounding what Camille recognized to be a forty-thousand-dollar bottle of champagne.

She stared at the tray, her lip upturned slightly in disgust before rolling her eyes and mumbling 'of course' under her breath. The waiter briefly appeared annoyed and ready to move on when she suddenly snatched a fluke. Her sudden motion nearly caused the young man to drop the tray, but he recovered quickly, his eyes forming into small slits as he glared at Camille.

She only shrugged, a smirk on full cinnamon-colored lips. The man huffed before hurrying in the direction of a middle-aged woman wrapped in a mink shawl, overdressed for the warm Alabama fall.

The trio stood at the top of the landing, far back enough to be hidden from view but close enough to watch the Coven's movers and shakers mingling below.

Armand stood off to the side watching Caesar and Evelyn; the two stood, their chests pressed together. His brother leaning forward to whisper in her ear. Annoyance ran through him, followed by a pang of jealousy, then more annoyance. Armand could picture Amelia and himself huddled together, sharing a joke that only the two of them understood.

Caesar laughed, "You know it's impolite to stare, brother."

Evelyn followed his gaze, her light brown eyes locking onto Armand's.

"Don't worry, Armand; soon enough, it will be you and Amelia." She added, teasing him. Her expression remained serious as her eyes shifted from a light brown to ashen grey. The smile she wore appeared more like a scowl.

Armand rolled his eyes, downing the amber liquid; to get through the night he needed something harder than the overpriced champagne. He tossed the empty glass into a far corner.

The couple separated; their hands still enclosed. Evelyn quickly checked her watch on her right wrist.

"It's time, dear." The remark was tossed casually over her shoulder, her playful tone from earlier gone.

"Of course business as usual. You ready, brother?" Caesar smirked at Armand.

He sighed annoyed, "let's get this over with. Are Mother and Father here?"

"Of course they are always present when the golden child is in town, but don't worry, they won't come out until later once all eyes are firmly on you," he chuckled, his eyes dark, "they want to make sure you shine."

"Fuck off, Caesar," Armand stated jokingly.

The lighthearted moment was over as the three approached the edge of the landing.

The DuBois brothers and Evelyn strode down the large staircase to rapturous applause. They moved as if they owned the place because they did, and neither took issue letting it be known to all present. They were the future of the Coven.

Caesar's fiancée was glowing, gliding down the stairs, her hand possessively in the crook of his arm. Armand wasn't Evelyn's biggest fan; she was arrogant, aloof, and at times rude, but she fit the part. Her bloodline was one of the oldest, and she came from one of the most prestigious families in the Chad Coven. The soon-to-be marriage was a gesture of good faith and an apology for past transgressions that were only mentioned in hushed conversations the DuBois children were never privy to join.

Armand noted how the richness of Evelyn's dark skin complimented his brother's olive tone. Few understood that blood wasn't the only part of the package so were looks. It was all about presentation. Aside from his brother's eagerness, those two were another reason he pushed for Caesar's accession over his own. The two were, aesthetically, as well as temperament-wise, the perfect couple.

At the bottom, the three paused waiting until the applause died down. Armand fought the urge to roll his eyes as he scanned the room; he stiffened when he gaze landed on Camille. She was off to herself; she raised her glass toward him. Armand could deduce from the glee in her eyes that his former lover was up to something. He wasn't sure how she was even in the building. Armand personally oversaw the guestlist ensuring it was crafted with great care. He made certain she wasn't on it.

His jaw clenched; *why did he agree to this?* Instinctively, he sought out an escape, then his eyes landed on her.

She was there with her mother and two of the young women he recognized from several days ago. He had dreamed about her for over a week, and she was glowing. Her hair was pulled back in a chignon and the dress hung off her shoulders, exposing flesh he imaged kissing.

The two made eye contact, and the scowl from his coming out party was gone, replaced with a smile that brightened her whole face. His breath hitched, and, for a second, he tried to remember all that he had seen in Spain and wondered if the ancient, pristine coasts were anything compared to her.

They were certainly not.

Armand had been so caught up in staring at Amelia he didn't hear his name being called and only came to when his brother shoved the microphone into his hand.

The elders of the council stared at him expectantly, the young women wantonly, his mother lovingly, but his father only glared his expression hard. The patriarch's eyes were a hazy deep yellow, a sign that he was angry. Armand could only speculate as to what he would be yelled at about later on once they were away from the watchful eyes of the Coven.

Never one for speeches, the eldest DuBois kept it short thanking everyone for their attendance before quickly handing the mic back to Caesar, allowing him to make the final remarks before they mingled with the crowd and before everyone took their seats for dinner.

Caesar and Evelyn were the first to enter the lion's den, their heads thrown back in laughter. The two made it look easy, and the jealousy from earlier was back; briefly, he wondered if he and Amelia could do the same.

He shook off the thought. The woman was entering his mind too frequently, making him nervous. He had never given much thought to any prospective conquest.

Once again, he scanned the crowd searching for her again. He nearly growled when Camille approached. She was in the mood to antagonize.

"Hi, Armand." She stated smirking, her eyes locked on to his.

He sighed, annoyed, "Camille." He moved to sidestep the model but stopped when she reached out, placing a slender hand on his belly. He stepped back, putting distance between them. Camille let her hand fall to her side.

"Now, that's not nice. I came in peace; despite, what happened we can still be friends."

Armand closed the gap between them, "Friends? Really? What do you want, better yet, why are you here? I don't recall your name being on the guest list."

She smiled; it was devilish, and Armand got the feeling there was something he didn't know. It was a feeling he didn't like.

"Really?" She feigned innocence, placing her hand on her chest, "well, luckily, I received my invitation; someone must have noticed the oversight and made the correction." She continued chuckling slightly. He was tempted to wipe the smirk off her face.

He was about to respond when he caught a glimpse of Amelia over Camille's shoulder. He didn't want to hope but could swear Amelia was looking at him. He was disappointed when she looked past him and started waving.

Four teens hurried toward her; they were giddy, and realization dawned on him that she wasn't seeking him out. Camille watched; the smirk only deepened as she watched his features go from anger to excitement before ending in disappointment.

"What's wrong? Amelia not fawning over you like the other mere mortals?"

His gaze shifted back to Camille, "stay away from her," he hissed.

"Calm down, I am over you. I have no interest in Amelia, I have new friend all my own. You should meet him." She looked around him and waved someone over.

"I don't have time for games; move and enjoy the evening."

"Armand, long time no see."

He paused bristling. The tall, dark-haired wolf knew the voice. It had been over fourteen years, and although the tone had deepened, he still knew it well. He turned, facing his former best friend.

"Cain," Armand spoke the name low, "I'm going to have to follow up with the coordinator and find out why low lives are being allowed in."

"Well, be sure to ask them why you're here." Cain took a swig of his drink.

"Oh, you two know each other?"

"Cut the shit, Camille," he spoke louder than intended, causing a couple to briefly stop their conversation and look at the trio.

Armand gave them a death glare and the two nodded before moving away from them.

"Why are you here?" Armand asked, stepping closer to Cain.

"Same as you. I came to be charitable. It's been some time since I have been out in polite society, but being set up for a rape and murder will make you a little leery of people. I'm sure you understand with you hiding in Spain and all."

Cain took another sip of his drink.

Armand was fuming and was about to respond.

"Don't worry, Armie, your secret is safe with me; besides, I came here to mingle with some beautiful lady. Maybe I'll find one to take home, but for the lucky lady, she won't end up like our dear Danielle."

He patted Armand on the shoulder, smiling before walking off and leaving him and Camille alone.

"You two should be careful." It was a veiled threat. Camille only smirked.

"No, Armie, you be careful." She giggled and turned, leaving him watching after her.

Caesar watched the exchange and decided to join his brother; Camille didn't disappoint.

"What was that?" Caesar asked, his eyes on Camille and Cain, "that looked rather intense."

Armand glanced at his brother before returning his gaze to the pair.

"Nothing," he hissed as he watched Cain stop and introduce himself to Amelia and the group of teens.

He moved to go after him but was stopped by Caesar placing a hand on his chest.

"That, brother, didn't look like nothing."

Armand remained silent, his breathing heavy, and Caesar followed his gaze over to Amelia and Cain.

"Look, brother; this is not the time nor place; besides, Amelia is a respectable woman. I doubt she'll go running off with another."

He chuckled.

Armand turned on him, knocking his brother's hand from his chest, "That's not what this is about. How did he get in?"

"Who? That guy?" Caesar pointed in Cain's direction.

Cain watched from his peripheral and slowly raised his glass toward the two brothers.

"Yes."

"My God, is that Cain? He certainly is a bit of an ass. Should I have security throw him out?"

"No, never mind." Armand turned, walking toward the opposite side of the room. Caesar watched his brother's retreating form before turning back to Cain. He would find out the man's motives, and if he presented as a roadblock, then the man would be eliminated.

The middle DuBois child sought out his sister Hera and headed in her direction. As she had only arrived a few hours ago, she would need to be brought up to speed on their brother and this potential threat.

He watched the three teens hang on to her every word and she theirs. Armand found their girlish laughter refreshing from the stiff and formal decorum of the Coven's esteemed members.

He found himself smiling and was about to take a sip of champagne when Cain came into view, causing the jovial moment to pass in haste. He growled low in his throat when the man approached Amelia for a second time tapping her playfully on the shoulder.

Cain placed a kiss on the back of her hand; he fought the urge to intervene. The interaction gave creep reminding him of his college year. The two years before Oxford were hazy, but he remembered that much about the man lurking around his woman.

His thoughts trailed at *his woman.*

The pair started to move, and Armand followed.

He stopped when he heard a high-pitched squeal and the image of his sister approaching; her arms outstretched as she came toward him. He sighed, stepping back to brace himself, and he had barely done so as his sister nearly jumped in his arms.

"I am so glad you are home." She whispered in the crook of his neck, and he chuckled at the sensation of her warm breath on his skin.

"I'm glad to see you too."

She let him go, stepping back to take him.

"Wow, why are you so tall." She pulled him in for another hug.

Many mumbled among themselves at the disruption but wouldn't voice their displeasure aloud, especially when that displeasure was the result of the alpha's only daughter. They soon turned their attention back to their drinks and stale conversation.

Armand didn't say much as he watched Cain and Amelia cross to the other side of the room over Hera's head.

Hera knew her brother's attention was elsewhere; Caesar had filled her in on the latest but failed to convey that their brother was, dare she say, madly in love. She stopped talking, merely watching him. It took him nearly a minute to realize she had stopped talking when he looked down at her.

"I'm sorry, sister; what were you saying?"

Hera smirked, "no, you're not. Looking for your lady," she poked him in the tummy playfully and practically skipped away before he could respond.

He brought his attention back to the area he had previously and found Amelia gone and Cain heading down the hall past the elevators.

Armand followed, waving off an approaching Council member, Reynolds Biltmore, as the old man wobbled in his direction.

Down a dark corridor, the man seemed to disappear, and he turned on his heel when he heard a door open.

"Are you following me now?"

Armand laughed nervously.

Amelia placed the paper towel in the trash by the door.

"Ah, no, I was back here…" he trailed off. He didn't have an excuse for lingering outside the women's restroom, and what came to mind would have sounded ridiculous, if not downright crazy.

She watched him, eyeing him up and down before laughing, "It's okay, your secret is safe with me."

He frowned playfully before smiling once again, "what secret?"

"You hate these things as much as I do, but because our families are attention-seeking and a tad bit sadist, we are required to be at these boring events. Now, there is nobody in there, and the window is large enough for you to shimmy through. If you want, since you are technically my alpha, I can give you a boost, but only at your request," she gave him a playful bow.

"You want me to shimmy through a window? And you'll give me a boost? Did I hear that correctly?"

"Yes, sir." She stood up straight, her hands at her side. The two collapsed into laughter.

Armand sighed, serious once again, "I thought I saw someone come back here. Someone that shouldn't be here. I am sorry to…" he gestured around, unsure of how to continue, "disturb you."

He sighed feeling like the chubby freshman in high school. He wasn't sure how to respond; part of him wanted to ask her to dinner, and the other half wanted to run for the window.

"No worries." She stated softly, her cheeks turning a dark ruby red. This was her first time flirting with a man, and she wasn't sure why she had or if she was doing it right. From first impression, she should hate him; he was arrogance personified. A part of her was nagging at her to run, but she didn't want to leave. Silence occupied the space between them.

"I...Amelia?"

"Yes, Armand," she spoke his name with a hint of seduction, her lips parted slightly, the pinkness of her tongue peeking through.

Armand felt arousal surge through him, and he had to remind himself that she was different. He wanted this to be different; she wasn't Camille. His arousal quickly left when the young model came to mind. He needed to find out why she and Cain were there.

"Dinner. Would you like to join me for dinner Friday?"

Reflexively, he held his breath.

She smiled, the nervousness and tension from before leaving as her shoulders relaxed, "yes, I would love to have dinner with you." The statement was spoken softly as long eyelashes bounced against brown tawny skin.

He sighed out of relief his body releasing the tension coiled within him from earlier. Camille and Cain forgotten.

"Great, it's a date. I mean, unless you don't want it to be, but it's just dinner." He stopped talking.

Amelia found the nervousness of the aloof and domineering man to be endearing and charming. She giggled out of habit and clamped her hand over her mouth at the utterance of the girlish sound. Both smiled and nodded before parting ways.

It was the first step to Armand's endgame. Their interaction made the night bearable for both. Armand's belly fluttered in anticipation as he would soon have his desires sated.

THE PAST.

His neck cramped but he ignored it. He watched and waited in the driver's seat of the tan Mazda. It wasn't his usual mode of transportation but for his purposes and when he need to remain hidden in the shadows it did the job.

He quickly sat up as he spotted Danielle walking out the front door of the sorority house no doubt headed to an early morning class. The rage from watching her sway back and forth with a frat boy the night before was gone replaced by excitement and anticipation.

Cain would wait until she rounded the corner before he exited the vehicle and followed.

In one swift motion he was outside the vehicle backpack on his shoulder. Like Danielle, he had an early morning class, in fact the same one. He had made sure of it with the casual sliding of two Benjamins across the counter. The clerk had eagerly snatched them up placing them in his breast pocket before mimicking Cain's actions and sliding the young woman's class schedule across the smooth surface.

The young man contemplated for weeks waiting for the perfect opportunity to introduce himself for a second time. The first encounter he had mumbled his name and as usual allowed Armand to bare the weight of conversation.

Among the humans, he had a much harder time although he fared no better with the young maidens of the Coven despite his wealth. He was Armand's sidekick. The Alfred to Batman. Almost all that knew him were unaware of his Wiltshire bloodline and his great aunt advised him to keep it that way. Before her passing, she had warned him of the dangers of dealing with anyone from the DuBois clan, but in his youth, he had been curious and genuinely formed a friendship with their alpha's eldest.

He sighed. He wouldn't bring up that up not now. Cain increased his pace and was nearly on her heels. Out of habit she had held the door open not bothering to look back and Cain seized the opportunity to touch her. A slight brush of his hand against hers was enough. She had been too distracted to notice. She was down the hall and once again out of reach.

"Excuse me," a young man hissed frustrated that his path was blocked. Cain mumbled an apology hurriedly moving to the side. He waited five

minutes before he followed after her. It would put him two minutes late, but he didn't mind. It would be at least another before their hungover TA arrived.

She felt eyes on her and lost focus during the lecture. It was the sensation of something crawling up her back that let her know she was being watched. Class was over and she hurried from the hall using the throes of glassed eyed classmates to lose him.

Danielle skipped the next glass opting to return to her room. She found more gifts and flowers this time placed at the foot of her bed along with a note.

I hope you enjoyed Hartford. Hopefully, I can join you next year. I would love to meet your mom and dad. - CL

She shuddered wondering how he knew she left to visit her parents in Vermont. Danielle gathered the items and placed them in the small closet along with the others. With a huff she decided it was time she did more than silently hoped he went away.

The flowers and cards were nice at first and initially she had brushed Cain off as a harmless observer, but his personality shifted. His efforts had grown bolder, and he made reference of claiming her in the last card she had received. It wasn't until she noticed Cain's presence in every class that she worked up the nerve to go to a professor. He listened as he wiped the Latin from the large chalk board before shuffling her off to a freshly seated dean.

The woman had listened nodding the dark green blank stare the only betrayal of the woman's annoyance.

"It's common for some young men to develop a type of infatuation with a woman that have an interest in pursuing. I assure you it's nothing dear. I am familiar with Cain; the boy is harmless and if what you say is correct and you have been ignoring him then he will go away eventually."

The dean rested her chin on her folded hands as she ran her eyes over Danielle.

"Forgive me for saying this but is there a reason you're not interested? From my understanding he comes from a very wealthy family, old money from down south. I am sure if you showed a little interest, it could be more than an infatuation. You're in our research program, correct? Maybe one day he could be a benefactor. You know curating a list of donors starts early during your academic career."

She raised her eyebrows hoping the young woman before her caught her meaning.

"No, he really creeps me out. There is no way I would go there." She sighed leaning back in the chair.

"Ok, but I am just saying a very wealthy young man could do a lot of things for an ambitious young woman like yourself. He's harmless but..." she through her hands up before re-arranging the photo frames on her desk, "if you're truly not interested talk to his friend Armand and have him talk to him. I am sure he can dissuade his attentions."

The dean began to re-arrange and shuffle papers on her desk before the older woman rolled over to the desktop and turned it on.

"Is there anything else?" She turned looking at her over dark rimmed glasses.

Danielle shook her head, "no, that's all. I'll talk to Armand maybe he can help."

The smile from the heavyset woman was strained as she nodded turning her attention to the computer as she typed in her password.

Danielle knew when she was getting the brush off and left the woman's office. Slowly she walked back to the sorority house each step felt heavy and she turned around several times out of habit. The junior couldn't shake the uneasy feeling of being watched.

She stopped her hand in her jacket pocket fingering the note Cain had left in her room. Although she had never seen him there, it wouldn't have been hard for him to get in. With the influx of young men in and out of the shared residence, she was sure he had been there at least twice. Her sorority sisters were too caught up in the game of pursuit by the future businessmen and heirs of fortunes to care that she felt unsafe. Danielle made a detour crossing the street and walking a block off campus to the bus stop.

The tan volleyball player had been correct in her assumption as a pair of dark green eyes watched. Cain followed, in his wolf form it was easy for him to stick to the shadows; he lost her when she bordered the bus.

He howled turning and heading back to campus and his car. The street was too busy for him to change, and an abandoned alley wasn't easily accessible.

Danielle arrived at the apartment and was surprised at how easy it was to get in. Armand answered after the third knock. He stood staring at her his expression more annoyed than the dean's had been.

He sighed opening the door further and motioning her in.

"Come in and have a seat."

He walked to the small kitchen leaving her alone as she took in the decor. It was well decorated the industrial and worn exterior not doing the chic and modern aesthetic of the inside justice.

He returned with a bottle of wine, two long-stem glasses and a soda.

"You have to forgive me, but I am expecting a guest soon so this will need to be quick." He sat across from her glancing at his watch.

"I won't be long, but we have to discuss your friend." She began popping the tab on the coke he had given her.

The sigh was long and strained as he whispered, "not again," under his breath. Armand pinched the bridge of his nose.

"He's following you, leaving gifts and notes?"

She only nodded a little nervous and worried that now it had been revealed that this was a pattern.

"I would say that he's harmless but," he stopped looking away briefly, "he's not outright dangerous but don't underestimate him. He's done this before. Cain isn't the most socially apt individual and when he finds someone he has an interest in unfortunately he doesn't know how to, for lack of a better word, pursue them in a proper fashion."

He was staring at her intently.

"I would say don't engage and eventually the infatuation will wear off. But in the meantime," he rose disappearing for the second time since she arrived.

He returned with a small sprayer in his hand and presented it to her. "Carry this."

She took the object reading the label, BEAR SPRAY was in bold letters on the side.

"Bear spray?" She asked looking afraid and confused.

He held up his hand, "don't ask questions just if you need to use it. I'm serious." His tone was sharp leaving no room for additional questions.

"Now, please leave. I will talk to him, but I can make no promises that he will stop."

Armand wanted the woman gone before Cain returned. He would misconstrue her presence as a sign he was interested, which for him wasn't the case.

She stood, placing the canister in her bag. She was near the door when Armand came rushing to her a small piece of paper in hand.

"This is my number call if you need me. Okay?" She nodded taking the note and placing it in her jean pocket.

Danielle left the apartment with no definitive solution but at least she had gotten further with Armand than she had with anyone else. Unlike the others he listened, and she had a feeling he wasn't telling her something; that a critical piece of information that might prove useful to her was missing.

Cain returned about to walk into the apartment building that he shared with Armand. There it was again; it was strong, and he followed. He crouched low as her scent grew stronger the closer, he got to the apartment.

It was mingled with that of another feminine odor as he approached he heard soft moaning. His breathing was heavy, and he considered breaking down the door and killing them both.

His canines were poking uncomfortably into the lower soft tissue of his mouth. Blood pooled at the edges of his gums, the liquid only fueling his rage. Cain slammed his head into the wall near the door. A woman and her small child stood to the side watching her arms wrapped protectively around the young boy.

"Sorry, sorry," he held up his hand as he staggered toward the elevator.

He pressed the lower floor heading for the building's basement. Once the metal doors were closed, he screamed.

"Fucking bitch!" He paced kicking at the sides of the elevator.

"I'll get you both," he leaned forward huffing, "don't worry Armand you'll pay for this."

Co-conspirator

Camille waited nearly forty-five minutes normally she wouldn't have stayed longer than fifteen, but the mysterious figure would reveal themselves tonight. Her phone rang and she pulled it from her pocket it was her mother.

She considered sending the call to voice mail but decided to answer.

"Mom now is not a good time," her tone harsher than necessary.

"You shouldn't speak to your mother that way. Warehouse downtown; you have the coordinates," the voice on the other end was that of a woman's but not her mother's and a wave of panic washed over her. A text came through, Camille looked at it before bringing the cell back to her ear.

"Why are you calling from my mother's number? I swear if you touch,"

She was cut off by the voice on the other end.

"Please no need for the dramatics," the woman's tone was bored, and Camille relaxed slightly.

"Your mother is more than safe she's still in Geneva. Will be until next Wednesday if I remember correctly. Warehouse thirty minutes don't be late."

The line went dead and slowly Camille stood up from the hood of her car. Quickly she slid into the driver's seat annoyance and anger made her want to give up the quest to unmask this conspirator. But she had come too far to let them remain hidden. She was in too deep to turn back, and she wasn't sure if she could.

Everything changed, no doubt, when she sought out Cain. The man's information did not come free and reneging on the deal she was sure could possibly get her killed.

Quickly, she unlocked the cell and dialed Gianna. She knew her sister wanted no further involvement, but she needed more information. A heavy feeling weighed on her that there were still missing pieces to this puzzle. She was willing to pay double even setup a meeting between her half-sister and their mother if that would entice Gianna to keep digging.

"What's up?" Gianna answered and Camille could hear two children screaming in the background. She rolled her eyes out habit.

"Cain. I need more info," Camille pushed the pedal harder speeding through a stop sign causing a small Porsche to honk wildly.

"I thought I told you to leave it alone, and besides what makes you think I want to keep digging. Boys, stop!"

"More money," she sighed tightening her grip on the wheel, "besides I need you; I need you to get this information for me. I am going to meet someone tonight."

"Tonight? Who? More importantly, why?"

"Yes tonight, Now. I don't know, and apparently they have been feeding me information on the DuBois clan."

"Wait! So you have been receiving dirt on the DuBois clan that you didn't ask for and you don't even know the who or why?"

Camille heard metal crashing as the silverware played its own tune, "no sounds more like you are being set up or walking into an ambush."

"I know that! Shit could go left tonight; I am aware!" she shouted banging her hands against the steering wheel.

"And you're still going?"

"Yes, I need to know who this person or people are. Wouldn't you want to know?"

Gianna sighed, "yes. Although I think what you are doing is the epitome of stupid, I have done worse. Keep your cell on. Do you have your locator turned on?"

"My what?"

"Wait let me grab my laptop." There was several seconds of shuffling and more banging in the background before Gianna returned.

"Ah, no you didn't have it turned on but don't worry. It's on now."

"How did you do that? You know what don't answer that."

"Fine, I wasn't going to. I will have a record of your movement in case shit goes left."

HER HEART RACED AS she turned off the engine and slowly exited the vehicle heading to the side door of the building. She looked around before grabbing the handle. Curiosity was gaining ground over logic and ultimately her inquisitive nature won, and she entered to find a man with his back turned.

Camille approached slowly her senses heightened. Her body was tight the fight or flight response kicked into overdrive as the hairs on her arms began to rise in anticipation. She planted her feet anchoring her 120 pound frame.

Her breath hitched. When he turned revealing chiseled features that were familiar.

"Caesar?" she whispered his name in disbelief questioning the image before her. She blinked hoping the successive flutters of her lashes would clear the imagery and reveal she had been hallucinating.

He held his arms out and up, "who else?" He chuckled darkly placing both hands back in his pockets.

"You're behind this?" Camille asked growing leery hoping she hadn't walked into a trap.

"I'm sure you're wondering why," he turned slightly looking at her before he inclined his head toward back of the spacious room.

"Come it's," he removed his hand from his left pocket and checked his watch, "late, well past dinner. Have you eaten?"

She slowly shook her head.

"Good, follow me, "he noticed her hesitation, "come, I can assure you are safe here; besides, you are a key part of the plan."

He raised his eyebrows smiling before dropping them and heading toward the door in the back of the warehouse.

She followed her eyes roaming the area all around her.

She entered to find Caesar and a woman sitting at a table. She quickly recognized the imposing African woman as Evelyn. The woman couldn't hide her shock and Evelyn laughed.

"She's adorable Caesar."

"Yes, she is dear but more than that she's our ticket to the top."

"Well, that depends if she holds her nerve," Evelyn stated staring at Camille chocolate irises dark, challenging.

The blonde quickly schooled her features and sat in the empty chair across from the couple.

"I can assume," she returned Evelyn's ice-cold stare, "that you were the one that called."

"I am," the dark-skinned woman stated her gaze boring into Camille's.

"Well, let's get to it, why did you bring me here?"

"Simple," Caesar now spoke as he reached for his fiancée's hand, "we came to talk business."

Camille leaned back in her chair her arms folded, "the floor is yours."

"As you very well know, Armand is set to take over by next spring."

She chuckled, "over Alpha Maximillian's dead body."

"That will happen sooner than you think."

Camille's brow wrinkled in confusion.

He held up his hand, "no need to give me that look, we are not going to murder my father, his illness is doing that for us albeit, slowly.

I have pulled his medical report; my father isn't aware that I know that the disease is progressing at an alarming rate which means the old man doesn't have much time. But..." he leaned back, "neither do we. We have to move fast and stroke the right fires pull the proper skeletons from the appropriate closets. That's where you come in, you understand?

"So, I am what lighter fluid?" Camille chuckled.

"So, you want to prevent Armand from becoming alpha, I get that. Your brother is an asshole but from all of the information you gave me it implicates your whole family going back to the Coven's origins. If it gets out your whole family burns and everyone tied to you." She glanced at Evelyn before focusing back on Caesar.

"So, I need to know why or else I'm pulling out."

Camille crossed her legs, "with the alpha dead and Armand ousted as the next male you take over as the Coven's head, but what's in it for me?"

"A council seat," he played with the tip of his tie.

She chuckled, "there are no women at the high table."

"Not yet," he uncrossed his legs.

It was Evelyn's turn to speak, "Caesar and I intend to usher in a new era, a more progressive era. It's time that we diversify place more women in strategic positions of power. Just think Camille, what being the first woman on the Council would do you for and not to mention your family."

"With us," Caesar interjected, "you can write your own destiny, no more existing in the shadows."

"I am sure that if you can get the other relics to agree to allow me on then I am indebted to you. Now how does that bring me out of the shadows so to speak?"

"No, you won't be indebted to us, but we would rely on your influence to help bring about this new era of change, but everything put before the Council would be ran through you of course; you will have first say as well as input."

Camille remained silent as she thought over the offer.

Evelyn and Caesar exchanged brief glances the seat was the carrot to ensure the young woman continued to comply and provide him details regarding Cain's intentions. He needed her to keep an eye on the mysterious man as the new addition hadn't originally been factored into his plans.

"I want a board seat as well. DuBois Enterprise."

Caesar sighed it was more than he was willing to offer but he figured she would never occupy the chair, "consider it done."

He leaned forward, "giving you and Armand's history, I won't announce until things fall more into place."

She smirked, "fine, but I need something from you two as well."

Evelyn laughed, "aside from what we are already giving you?"

"Yes, small in comparison to the fact I am doing the leg work to give you two the world."

"What is it you need?" Caesar asked.

"Cain. You know he's a Wiltshire, he wants revenge against the DuBois, something about a stolen dynasty. So, I don't think a council seat will placate a man who believes he's a king in search of his stolen kingdom. Also, I need information a lot more than I can get. I need to know more about that family and who I am working with."

"I wasn't aware that Cain was a Wiltshire, that complicates things," he looked over at Evelyn before bringing his attention back to Camille, "you will have what you need, expect a call in about a week."

Camille nodded.

She didn't eat much picking at her food for show. Camille occasionally placed a cube of meat in her mouth. Not that the couple across from her noticed. They were too enthralled with one another and the bright future that awaited them.

She wanted Armand to suffer but what Caesar and Evelyn were proposing was treason of biblical proportions. He was turning on his brother and that meant he couldn't be trusted. But their offer was appealing. A seat on both the Council and the company board would propel her further than anyone in her family would have imagined. Since the hope of her one day becoming Armand's bride was dashed, she needed other means of elevation and the two in front of her might prove to be the way.

After the final course was finished the three shared a glass of wine and moved to more friendly topics with the two speaking of wedding arrangements. It was nearing midnight when they parted ways. Camille still not fully at ease with what she was agreeing to participate in doing.

Evelyn and Caesar slid in the backseat of the SUV the driver quickly moved to get behind the wheel. Tim sped out of the warehouse heading toward the couple's penthouse downtown.

"Do you think she's solid?" Evelyn asked as the streetlights illuminated her dark skin causing it to have an iridescent glow.

"Yes and...no. I think she'll go along with this for a while then she'll have a change of heart. By that time, it'll be too late and then we can dispose of her." He stated placing a kiss on the back her hand.

She smiled before it faltered, "and Cain? He may prove more of an obstacle than anticipated."

"It's simple enough to deal with Cain. He wants a seat at the table. Power. His axe to grind is with my brother, not us. I'll set up a meeting with him. He, my dear, may prove to be an asset after all. After Camille serves her purpose then Cain can finish the rest, then we finish Cain for regicide."

"But how do we make sure we are not caught in the crosshairs?"

She asked bringing her gaze from the passing scenery to him.

He offered her a sly smile, "I think our plan is solid. Tomorrow my father will receive a package and from there the ball should really start to roll then."

"Should? You know I don't like uncertainty."

"Will, dearest, will."

The two chuckled as Tim guided the car into the parking garage of the apartment building.

IT'S NEARLY 1 AM NORMALLY she would wait until a decent hour to call but she needed someone to talk besides she doubted if her sister would be asleep at this hour. She quickly pulled up Gianna's number.

Her sister's voice was groggy, and Camille hissed out of unwarranted frustration.

"Hello?"

"I thought you were going to wait up for me." She stated her tone dry.

"Oh shit Camille, I didn't expect this meeting to turn into an all-night thing. This couldn't wait until morning or the afternoon. Besides, what took so long?"

She could hear the other woman shift on the other end.

"We had dinner and talked."

"Why are you in bed you're part wolf I thought you'd be up."

"Honey when you've got four kids that night wolf shit goes out the window real quick. Now tell me about the meeting or I'm hanging up."

She sighed, "Caesar and Evelyn."

Gianna groaned, "the GQ couple... now I know you need to leave this shit alone."

"No, I am not going to leave it alone. Anyway, you said be careful."

"Same thing. Now what's happened and it must be big if you are calling me at this ungodly hour."

Camille plopped down on the edge of the bed.

"I have been getting information about the family, you know back alley business dealings, hidden accounts, the works. I am not sure if I mentioned that part."

"No, you didn't."

"It's bad information heavy shit that could topple a dynasty. Shit that I don't think even you would have been able to find. Caesar is plotting to take down Armand."

She blurted everything out her hand over her face.

Gianna remained silent on the other end; this was heavy. She had read about coups but never witnessed one. This branch of the Coven was new and something like this would destabilize an already precarious experiment that frankly was still in its infancy.

Camille knew the other woman was right. Although she wouldn't admit it out loud.

Gianna huffed trying to calm herself down her hands were shaking, "well, did they say why? You know what...don't answer that I'm coming over."

The line went dead before Camille could respond.

Within thirty minutes there was a buzz at the gate and Camille headed downstairs.

Her sister barged in hand on her hip face a dark plum.

"Are you out of your damn mind?"

"Well, hello to you too. Damn that was fast. Besides I'm not sure."

Camille shut the door and followed Gianna into the kitchen.

She sat at the bar as she watched the older woman open cabinets and raid her fridge pulling out an expensive bottle of wine that was gifted her.

Gianna pulled two wine glasses from the cabinet and placed them on the counter with a thud. Camille cringed before she relaxed and took a deep breath.

"Is this bothering you?" Gianna asked smirking.

"Yes, those are very rare crystal glasses imported from Tahiti." She drummed her fingers against the counter as she spoke.

"Well," she chuckled noticing Camille was tensing up again, "I'll be more careful, unlike you." She sighed pushing the other glass toward the host.

Camille snatched it up and downed the liquid in two large gulps. She held it up silently asking for another. Gianna quickly complied this time filling the hollow bulb just below the rim.

Gianna sat on the stool next to her.

"So, start from the beginning."

Camille wasn't sure what made her tell all. Maybe it was because no one else was more aware of the situation other than the parties involved and she needed an unbiased opinion as well as a sounding board.

Gianna listened intently part of her was concerned she had that nagging feeling the young woman was being naïve and was playing a highly dangerous game. But another part of her was curious as to why she cared. Due to her half-blood status, she would never be taken in by their mother nor the coven.

They made that very clear ten years ago when she tried to join.

So, what if they took down the arrogant little snob and why did she care if her equally arrogant and snobbish sister got hurt in the process.

Camille finally stopped talking and stared out the window at the rising sun.

Gianna sat running over the details in her head it was a lot of information to process.

"This sounds like a set up."

"Why do you say that?" Camille shifted her gaze and was now staring at her. The irises of her eyes had taken on a lime green hue and Gianna had to look away briefly.

"Well, I doubt if those two are going to come in and buck tradition especially after removing his brother. Sounds like they want you as a patsy. The offer seems too good to be true but then again, they could be sincere. It's hard to say. What's your gut telling you?"

Camille brought her focus to the countertop before refocusing on Gianna, "honestly, I don't know. A part of me would love to be able to sit on the board and help bring in some real change. But..." she trailed off unsure of herself.

"This started out as a way to get back at Armand now I am not so sure. This is getting..."

"Scary?"

Camille didn't speak; she simply nodded.

"It should be, I have investigated cover ups and hostile takeovers, conflicts among families that have led to murder. With all you have told me let me do some more digging. I want you to be fully aware of the deal you've entered with the devil."

Threats and Revelations

It was nearing the hour when the black SUV pulled up. Maximillian sat back fingering the vial and the note. It wasn't the same, but it was eerily similar even Madame Nikki's insignia was etched into the glass in black ink. He held it up in the florescent glow of the streetlight.

His phone vibrated and he slowly removed it from his pocket. It was Hemesh and he considered sending her to voicemail but decided to take the call. He was about to answer when he spotted the headlights of a car pull into the alley behind the abandoned building.

He dismissed the call throwing the phone onto the seat. Quickly he exited the vehicle John remained inside his eyes firmly on his alpha.

Charles did the same nearly running to Maximillian.

"Did you get one too?" Charles asked looking around.

"Quiet down," Maximillian hissed scanning the area.

"Fuck that! When we did this, you said no one else would know, there would be no blow back."

"You were well aware of the consequences and all of the possible outcomes." The six-foot man pointed his finger in the face of the slightly shorter, older council chairman. He was starting to get angry as Charles' hysteria grew.

"No, you promised you damned near guaranteed that we were in the clear. You said I was the only one you talked to," he pulled the note and a small vial identical to the one Maximillian had in his pocket holding it up in Maximillian's line of sight.

"Someone else knows and I doubt if it's Madame Nikki. She's been dead for over thirty years, I saw to that," he raised an eyebrow.

Maximillian sighed, "and we made sure her family was well compensated. You can't hold onto the guilt from this, you have to let it go."

He reached out and grabbed his shoulder with his free hand. Charles quickly shook him off.

"Don't touch me!" He shouted.

"Calm down." Max held up his hand, "tell me what else you received? Was it a note?"

Charles reached again into the pocket of his blazer and pulled out a photo and held it up.

"No, they sent this."

It was photo of Armand and Amelia at the gala, the two were alone. Maximillian reached for the photo his heart began to race. He had done many things to protect his family only for his son to become a target.

He rubbed his thumb over the photo. The young man looked unsure but happy the hard expression he wore like a mask gone enhancing the softness of cocoa eyes.

"Read the back," Charles whispered watching his childhood friend carefully. He locked eyes with the doctor and slowly turned it over.

His eyes quickly scanned the back his mouth falling slightly agape. He brought his eyes up to rest on Charles.

"Yeah, you stay calm."

"Is this all that you received?"

Charles took a deep breath and slowly blew out the breath in a gush of air.

"No, before today I received the autopsy report for Samuel with a note that says, 'we know' and 'accomplice' written in pig's blood."

"Okay, anything else?"

"Yes, someone sent me a copy of the original decree we all signed and the other one we," he stepped closer, "forged."

"Damnit! Why didn't you tell me before now?"

"I thought it was you."

"Why would I send you that?"

"I thought it was because of Amelia and Armand."

"No, I don't involve myself with whom my son's screws."

"It's more than that and you know it. Besides we have an agreement, and had you made him stay the two of them would have been married a hell of lot earlier and maybe we wouldn't be standing here discussing some shit that happened thirty years ago!"

"He wasn't ready. I wasn't about to force my son to marry a girl he didn't know. This way is better let them give it a try and if he loses interest, we can say we tried."

Maximillian waved his hand nonchalantly his forehead as well as his palms were damp.

"I think it's more than that. If it isn't, you will honor our deal and order him to marry her. I will not allow your son to use my daughter as a whore like he's done with all the others."

"You, your wife, sons, and Amelia are all ambitious. I will not allow my son to get caught up in you and your family's schemes."

"There is no scheming Max, remember Darsh is dead and so is Samira, Samuel and all the others that knew and anyone that suspected our involvement. You and I made a deal. Your son and my daughter."

Maximillian thought for a moment, "it's been too long. The deal is off."

Charles chuckled "no, you owe me Max. You owe me big."

"No, I don't owe you shit."

"No, Max, you owe me everything! Your son will marry Amelia that is what we agreed to, if you back out of this there will be consequences!"

"Bullshit, you don't threaten me. Remember yourself I am your alpha!"

"Fuck you, Max! Remember yourself! You wouldn't have the seat you currently occupy had I not went along with your shit, so you have some respect!"

The two friends were near blows and stood only inches apart both fighting the urge to shift.

Charles hissed causing Maximillian to bare his canines. Charles' dark skin glowed under the dim alley lights, and he stepped back. There were better ways to deal with his old friend.

The thin blonde hairs on Maximillian's arms loss their stiffness falling flat against damp skin. He had no will left to fight.

"Make it happen Max! That much I am due." Charles turned heading for his car.

The alpha only watched as Charles speed out of the alley.

CHARLES TORE THROUGH the threshold of the bedroom. Diane slowly sat up the book she was reading casually placed beside her.

He stood looking down at her only holding up the photo as his only greeting.

Diane gasped when the image and the two bodies became clear in her field of vision.

"Did you know about this?" Charles hissed his large hands shaking slightly and he bore into Diane with round deep almond-colored eyes.

She was in front on him in a flash snatching the photo from his hand. It was of their daughter and Armand. The young woman's head back the man along with her wore the same expression except his eyes were open, intense, and locked onto the woman standing only a few feet from him.

Any other man and Diane would have been livid, but it was Armand, and she placed her hand over her gaping mouth to stifle a laugh of joy.

Charles was confused and furious. It was too soon; he had yet to secure the engagement with Max, and the boy was too fickle to rely on traditional means of courtship.

"What Diane? This is serious," the look he gave her was strange and Diane was shaking from silent laughter at the moment unconcerned that her husband was upset.

"This is great! They are talking to one another. He has his sights set on her. You should be happy; we don't have twist arms here."

"No, we might. Maximillian doesn't want to hold up his end of the bargain."

Diane stopped laughing and sighed.

"This was my greatest fear, Charles. You push too hard at times. Where did you go tonight?"

He sighed, "I met with Max after I received this," he pointed to the photo in her hands, "someone is stalking them. Someone that knows what we did all those years ago."

"I don't understand love." Her eyes were soft, and she reached for his hand. She had been curious as to the tension and secrecy surrounding their alpha and her husband but had brushed it off just as she had done with many inconveniences in her life.

Tentatively, he reached for his wife's shoulders giving them a light squeeze hoping the action would in some way give him the courage to state his thoughts aloud.

"Diane, sit," he gestured toward the bed guiding her over to it as he sat next to her.

"I wanted to isolate you from this but, when Amelia was young, I made an exchange with Max. His son, his eldest and mine. I made him promise a union between Armand and Amelia. I wanted those two to be married to put our bloodline in the path to become alpha."

Diane dropped the photo, her eyes dark as her husband continued to explain. It was only out of curiosity that she didn't start shouting at him.

"I did something for him. Something that if it were to get out would destroy me, us. All of us."

"What..."

He raised his index finger gently placing it against her bottom lip.

"Please listen, if I don't get this out, I think I'll go crazy Diane, my misdeeds are starting to come calling and I don't know what to do."

The anger that had been building evaporated like dew on an Alabama summer morning and Diane placed her hand over the shaking one resting on his knee. She had never seen him like this.

"Charles, what did you do? Please, tell me." Her voice was soft, and Charles wanted to lean in but was afraid at what would happen if he revealed all.

"I killed someone. Some people."

She let out a slow breath as she quickly drew in another. She had her suspicions and a nagging feeling that somehow Samuel, Samira, Hemesh, and Maximillian all played a part along with her husband in whatever this was. Diane just wasn't sure.

"Who did you kill and why? Surely, it can't be that bad."

"But it is," he forced through clenched teeth.

"Samuel, Diane."

She scoffed, "how? Look Max issued the challenge, Samuel accepted, it was all above board. He happened to be weak at the time so..." she trailed off as the events from before started to trickle in. They were just drops. A piece of paper here a whispered conversation there but it was starting to paint a vivid picture.

"A week before Samuel came to you for a checkup. I remember because you were nervous. You've never been nervous before although I knew you were terrified of the man, we all were. I will ask you again Charles what did you do?"

A light sheen of moisture glistened in the chandelier light making the man's forehead appear large and uneven, his palms were soaked.

"I injected him with…something. I don't know what, we got it from a lady or rather Max did. Some half breed witch. The deal was for me to give him the shot, Max would challenge, and my hands would be clean of it." He hissed as if burn by the revelation and the lie he repeated to himself.

He was rocking slightly from side to side. The trouble of a guilty conscious was that it made one restless and Diane looked on a in a mixture of horror and pity.

"Don't feel bad dear. We all have our secrets."

"Not like this D. Not like this."

She sighed unsure whether she should reveal her misdeed and that of her longtime friend.

"Look, it's not like my hands are entirely clean. I helped Hemesh dispose of a body."

Charles regarded her, "a random dead body isn't the same."

"Worse, it was her sister."

His eyes bucked in horror, and he had turned an ashen grey. Diane was afraid he would pass out.

He groaned as his hand flew to cover his face.

"Oh my God, forgive me," he sobbed.

"What is it? Please."

"Max went along with all of this because he thought Samuel killed Samira, I wasn't going to do it but when her body was found Max assumed it was him. Oh my God when he finds out he's going to kill her you know that?"

"You can't tell. Are you going to tell him?"

He sighed his face tear stained and sweaty.

"No, unless I have to, but Hemesh has done no ill toward us from what it sounds like she wants Amelia and Armand together."

"Yes, she does." She scooted closer slinking an arm around his mid-section.

"Don't worry, we will get through this," she whispered against his neck.

GIANNA LEFT CAMILLE'S worried and although she hated to admit she was afraid. She had dealt with cases of cover ups before. Although they were usually disputes over money or the occasional sibling rivalry between the children of the father's current and ex-wives. Nothing like this.

The long-time private investigator previously only dealt with humans. It was easier and she felt she could handle herself if things took a turn and they decided to come after her but this was different.

She was going up against a powerful and hidden force that operated in the shadows, but curiosity was her fuel. She wanted, needed to know more; her life had been altered by them.

The middle-aged woman sighed as she rounded the curve. She quickly gazed at the mansions that littered the exclusive suburb. A ping of jealousy flared. Camille had grown up in a place like this the best of everything never knowing nor understanding what real hard work felt like.

Unlike Camille, everything the mother of four had was the result of a long hard fight. She had only met their mother once over lunch. Elizabeth had been friendly, understanding but made it clear further contact was not an option. As a young college student juggling two jobs she had reluctantly expected the money offered to stay away.

The three million that sat in her account felt like an act of treason on her part.

MAXIMILLIAN WAS NEARLY done reading his article on the New York Times site when John entered carrying an envelope. The bald man stood his shoulders back and hand by his side.

"Yes," he drawled not bothering to look up from the iPad next to his plate.

"Sir, a letter arrived for you by carrier a few moments ago. It has no sender shall I return it?"

Maximillian held out his hand, "no I'll take it thanks John."

The valet approached and handed him the envelope before giving a slight bow and standing off to the side always in ear shot.

Hemesh entered pulling her robe around her petite frame.

"Good morning, dear."

Maximillian let out a small grunt.

Hemesh stopped and eyeballed her husband of thirty-five years.

"That's it? I worked very hard last night to make sure you had a good morning." She sat her expression now playful.

He looked over the rim of his glasses at her.

"Good morning dear, and yes it's a good morning but last night was better." He winked at her and Hemesh blushed turning her lightly browned cheeks a light saffron. She breath deep as she ran her hand through sable colored hair.

The alpha's heart skipped a beat as he was reminded of Samira.

He looked down out of shame. After all these years he still couldn't shake the feelings he had for the deceased woman. He felt guilt as he believed it was his fault that her life was cut short.

Hemesh's smile faltered at his shift in mood and could only speculate he was thinking of her older sister. She sighed before nodding at the maid to serve breakfast.

Before long Maximillian excused himself from the table sparing his wife a quick glance as he left the room. His valet on his heels.

Hemesh sat sipping at her coffee before waving over Natalia.

The six one brunette bent forward her face level with that of her employer.

"Find out what my husband is hiding." Hemesh whispered the command in Natalia's ear. Her only response was a small nod as she stood tall and quickly left to carry out her task.

"YOU WERE VERY RUDE to the Reynolds and Piersons. What's the point of going to dinner if you aren't going to listen to them?"

Hemesh asked annoyed as she started removing her jewelry.

Maximillian disappeared into the large walk-in before returning.

"I received these this morning."

He held up the papers and Hemesh rolled her eyes. "That's why I wasn't talkative over breakfast and later I found out more information the reason I wasn't at my best this evening."

"So, you got bad news. You've never let it interfere before. Do you want the Council to start questioning your temperament to lead?"

Her shoulders slumped; she wouldn't criticize not tonight. "I'm sorry with everything that is going on you don't deserve me dumping on you too. What is it about?" She nodded at the papers.

"Samira." The named was whispered and Hemesh rolled her eyes as she nearly ripped the sapphire from her ear.

"It's because of her."

He held them towards her so she could read the heading. Hemesh leaned forward slightly trying to focus in on the small type font. She made out the words 'autopsy report' before she closed her eyes sighing.

"Really?" She turned back to her vanity and sat down in a huff, "I'm always in the shadows, a dead woman's shadow." She spoke softly placing her head in her hands.

"What are you talking about? You're not in anybody's shadow Hemesh, and yes really Hemesh, if this gets to the council or to the board of trustees everything is over, finished!"

She stood up abruptly knocking over the bench.

"Get over her! She's dead Max, dead. He killed her! Was it because of you who knows? For all I know you could have done it! Did you kill my sister?!" She shouted pointing at him.

He looked affronted, "You know me! I would never; I loved her!"

"And still do apparently! Why can't you get over her? Am I not enough, haven't I given enough?" She was angry and on the verge of tears.

"I love you too. I love you, Hemesh what more do you need?"

"For you to get over her, that's what I need. Instead of us spending the last bit of time we have left together you are waving around autopsy reports and whispering the name of a dead woman. She's gone Max. She's no more and hasn't been for a long time."

"I'm sorry I loved her from afar and if I had my way then yes, I would have married her." He looked at her solemn as he shared his hidden desire to the woman that had given him a large portion of her life not to mention her love and loyalty; as a mate he could not have asked for more.

She hmphed roughly wiping at the tears cascading down her cheeks, "save your lies for the council tomorrow."

"What do you mean? I do not wish to fight." He moved toward her only for her to step back holding up her hands.

"Samira was pregnant Max with your child. I doubt that can happen from loving someone from afar."

He stood shocked crumbling the papers in his left hand. His body had grown tense and he fought hard against the tears that were threatening to fall. Had he known he would have protected her better hidden her away.

"How?" He lost the battle, and his cheeks became damp, and he brought his hand up to his chest for the second time that evening. The pain was near unbearable.

"Well, dear, I imagine the same why I got Armand, Caesar and Hera, you pounding away for fifteen minutes?" She chuckled, "I have always known about you two. Oddly enough out of the two people I have loved the most only Darsh had the courage to tell me the truth. I suppose my late brother didn't want me walking around like a fool."

She continued, "don't be upset with him, I already knew about the baby. You see Samira was terrified, being promised to Samuel as a virgin and yet carrying another man's child. I am assuming he found out somehow. Maybe that's why he killed her."

Maximillian stood quiet the papers forgotten by his side. Had he known he would have done something. What, he wasn't sure but given how much he loved Samira it would have been a no brainer.

He would have left taken her and their child with him. He would have left his son and Hemesh with the knowledge that Darsh would have done the right thing and provided for his younger sister and nephew.

"Why didn't you say something? I would have stopped had you asked," he whispered, "I am so sorry."

Hemesh stared at him feeling the same annoyance for her husband that she had felt for her sister all those years ago. Momentarily, she wondered has easy it would be to get rid of him as well.

"Don't apologize and above all don't lie, at least not to me, it's over. All of that died with Samira and Samuel."

He held up the papers, "I am afraid not. Someone knows and now Armand will pay the price; all of them will."

He dropped the crumbled sheets into the trash bin, "I have sent for Hera to return home and for the time being I will have Caesar and Evelyn move into the penthouse on the twenty-first floor. As for Armand he'll take more convincing to get him here and to get him to stay."

"That's the Spenser's penthouse."

"Well, they will have to move!" he shouted, "this is not the time for decorum, Hemesh our children are in danger!"

She sighed not having the will to argue further, "you're right, habit of mine. I apologize. We shouldn't fight." She stood walking to him and placing her arms around him.

"Tell me what has happened? Who knows?"

He explained about the papers that had arrived in the last few months and he had to give details regarding the plot to remove Samuel but kept certain details surrounding the disappearance of Madame Nikki and a few others to himself.

He figured the less his wife knew the safer she would ultimately be.

HEMESH WOKE TO FIND the space her husband normally occupied empty. She sat up scanning the room. When he was troubled she would normally find him staring out the large window overlooking the city. When she didn't spot him in his usual place by the large window she rose peeling down the cotton sheets that clung to her damp skin. Hemesh grabbed her robe from the foot of the bed and placed it on her nude frame.

Slowly, she descended the stairs the light from his first floor office drew her attention and she entered to find him slumped over the desk asleep. The papers he had placed in the trash from earlier crumpled in his fist.

The DuBois matriarch's eyes grew watery as she approached and placed a soft kiss on his temple.

"I know, I loved her too."

Hemesh

The past.

The voice on the other end was strained and the person sounded out of breath. Diane pushed the receiver closer into her ear and repeated a hesitant 'hello?' Another strangled cry and more hyperventilating followed.

Diane handed the small child off to the nanny and placed her hand on her hip, "who is this? I'm hanging up."

"Wait!"

Diane pulled the phone back before placing it back at her ear.

"Hemesh? Darling what's wrong?"

"I..." she trailed off and Diane sensed something wasn't right. Her friend had never been so distraught.

"Say no more where are you?" The question was answered with silence and the young mother decided to keep probing until she had her friend's whereabouts.

"Hemesh, listen where are you? I can't help you if I don't know where to find you." She stated and waited patiently.

After nearly a minute the caller spoke, "I'm at home, Max isn't here but he will be soon and I...I don't know what to do." She was becoming frantic.

"I knew about them, but I thought with the engagement she would stop. I just thought they would stop. Then she told me."

"Told you what? Hemesh you aren't making any sense. Who is this she?" Diane picked up the phone cradle and took a seat on the sofa. She was worried.

"Samira. I've always known they were sleeping together. Her and Max but Diane I didn't mind," her voice was soft, and Diane feared her young Indian friend was on the verge of a breakdown.

"But then she told me that she was keeping it and was going to tell Max. She wanted to rip apart my family."

"Calm down, tell me what happened."

"The baby Diane, the baby. She was going to tell him." Sobbing was heard on the other end. Diane sighed she felt for the new mother.

"Hemesh darling don't get too upset. These things happen. I'll tell you a little secret. Charles has a two-year-old he doesn't think I know about. An outside child isn't uncommon. Honey, it comes with the territory so to speak."

Diane knew her words weren't much comfort, but she hoped what she said would help. When her own mother told her those exact words it dulled the pain if only temporary.

"No, this wasn't some random whore. D, my sister, and you don't know Max. He loves her so much. So, I had to do it. I had to take a stand she wouldn't stop she was so mean the things she said."

Hemesh broke down. Her sobbing was loud, and Diane momentarily placed the receiver on her chest. A part of her was truly sad but she didn't have all day to console the woman, normally she would have spoken a few words of solace and ended the call, but something nagged at her that it was important she stayed on the line.

Realization dawned on her, "Hemesh sweetie, what did you do?"

What followed was more sniffles then she responded, "I killed her."

1 hour before the call

Samira had agonized the previous night regarding the decision she had made and what she decided she would do next. It was early and she wanted to catch them both at breakfast as she pulled up to the large colonial style home.

She parked and made the small trek to the front door. The Tuscan double doors had an Ebony finish and Samira remembered being jealous that her sister got to design the home of her dreams with the man she loved.

She knocked hard jumping slightly at the sound of bone colliding with wood. It was faint a voice saying "I'm coming" was heard and Samira held her breath when she realized it was Hemesh.

She took a deep breath as the door opened revealing a rosy cheeked Hemesh carrying her nephew. Another pang of jealousy hit her, and she felt lightheaded.

Hemesh smiled offering her free arm for an embrace. Samira wanted to shrink into the floor.

"Come in please," Hemesh pulled her over the threshold and into the large open foyer.

"What brings you over? And so early?" She turned heading toward the first level kitchen.

Samira followed behind her. The pregnant woman's resolve was beginning to falter it had to be soon or else she feared she would not go through with it.

They arrived at the center aisle and Armand was placed in a highchair. The two sisters sat across from one another. Hemesh rose quickly and went to the cabinet to grab two coffee cups.

"Coffee?" She causally through over her shoulder as she started pouring them a cup of the dark brown brew.

She placed the cups in front of them and sat down once again looking at her sister expectantly.

"Well, what brings you over?" Hemesh asked taking a sip.

Samira sighed collecting herself.

Hemesh noted her distress and quickly placed down the ceramic mug. "Is everything okay?"

"No, I was hoping to catch you and Maximillian, is he around by chance?

The younger of the two sat up straighter tensing, "no, he had to leave early this morning for business he said. Why? What does this have to do with him?"

She licked her lips tasting the bitterness of the berry red lipstick.

"It has everything to do with him actually."

Hemesh looked over at Armand he was sleeping his head flopped over to the side and drool coated his chin.

"Maybe I should have said something a few years ago. I know about you and Max," she whispered her eyes had grown watery, "and I forgive you. There is no need to confess." Her cheeks were damp.

"No, I am not here for your forgiveness Hemesh but, I am glad you know half of the story. I'm pregnant and it's Max's." She stated her hands had begun to shake so she placed them in her lap.

Hemesh's face fell, and she stood.

"Why would you do that? You're engaged to Samuel, both of you are idiots!" She hissed placing her hands to her face, "oh my God, he's going to kill all of us! You have to get rid of it before he finds out."

Samira sat in silence watching as her sister spun in a circle before she collapsed on the bar stool. It took a minute for the implication to sink in but when it did Hemesh's eyes came aglow, and she stared at her sister.

"You're here to tell him, aren't you? You want to take him away?"

Samira sighed, she would have to harsher with her sister than she initially intended, "Hemie, let's be honest, he was never yours in the beginning. If it wasn't for Father, you and Max would have never been married. You know this."

Hemesh eyes were watery as her sister spoke the truth, if wasn't for the blood oath between the fathers, theirs and that of Samuel's, Samira would have been free to marry Max and she would have ended up with nothing. Her greatest fear was at her counter. Her sister had come to lay claim to her long-time secret love.

"Don't call me that you lying bitch!" Hemesh spat out her cheeks damp. She becoming more upset as her mind raced.

"We don't have to get irate Hemesh please. Armand," she gestured toward her nephew in hopes that it would quell the young mother's rising hysteria.

"Don't make this about him! You weren't thinking about him when you screwing my husband. Why are you doing this? What do you hope to gain by ripping my family apart? What about the alpha? Samuel will not stand for this; do you expect him to stand by while he is humiliated by the two of you?"

"No, my intentions were not to harm you. This thing between Max and I have been going on longer than the two of you have been together. I came for the man I love. I am carrying his child. I want a family Hemesh."

"You will have a family."

"No, not with him. I refuse. I want the man I have always loved you must understand. What if you were in my position?" Samira's eyes were pleading for understanding.

Hemesh stared at the countertop she was in a hurricane of emotion.

"But I love him too. Always have." She wiped her cheeks with the back of sweatshirt sleeve.

Hemesh couldn't remember when she picked up the knife, she had used to cut up cubes of raw meat for her son. She remembered the way the flesh gave way under the steel point as it penetrated skin and chipped away bone. Her hearing had tuned, and she flinched at the faint snap of the collar bone.

She felt her sister tense as she was caught in the early stages of the change no doubt a reflex to the shift in energy. Hemesh held her sister her eyes locked onto hers. They were watery and wide in disbelief. Pain had yet to register and Hemesh took the opportunity to push the blade in further giving it a slight twist.

The grey Yale sweatshirt was now dark, and the smell of blood was thick in the air. Slowly she guided her to the floor where she straddled her and snatched the blade from the woman's upper chest.

Samira gurgled. She tried to speak plead with her baby sister, but blood replaced words and she could only stare as she watched her sister raise the knife above her head before Hemesh brought it down driving it into the center of her chest.

She stood looking over at her son and wondered how he could have slept through everything. Her mind quickly went to the maids and the nanny. They would be here within the next two hours, so she had to move fast.

She would need help moving the body and with cleaning. Maximilian would be heartbroken so would their mother. Quickly she removed her top, pants and slippers kicking them near the body. Those would have to go.

She grabbed the dish rag and frantically searched under the cabinet grabbing the bottle of ammonia. She cleaned rubbing down the whole kitchen nearing choking from the noxious fumes in the process.

Armand began to cry no doubt the smell was the culprit to the end of a peaceful slumber, and she picked him up soothing him as she carried him upstairs. Hemesh returned this time with a large blanket in her arms.

Relief washed over her as she made quick work of wrapping her sister in the softness of the cashmere whispering a prayer as she covered the young woman's head.

Restless

"My love!" Caesar called out entering the large apartment. He had just ended a call with his Father upset that they would have to move.

"In here!" Evelyn's voice rang out and Caesar followed the sound to the sitting room. His movements slowed as he heard and picked up on the scent of others aside from those of the Evelyn and the few staff they employed.

He rounded the corner to find his future in-laws. Evelyn's father stood extending his hand. Caesar took it giving it a firm shake before he sitting next to Evelyn.

Hamid began his gaze shifting from his wife to the couple in front of him. Finally dark irises settled on Caesar.

"My daughter tells me you are closer to establishing the Federation. How did you bring your father on board of such a venture? He has been against an international league for years, but I have great respect for him and his opinion in this matter. When your former alpha Samuel insulted our delegation, it was Maximillian who reached out to make amends. He even arranged this," he gestured toward the couple.

Caesar lovingly took Evelyn's hand, "and I am forever grateful to you and my father for arranging such a union."

He inclined his head as a sign of respect and Caesar did the same. Although he rattled his brain for an answer to his soon to be father in-law's question.

"It took some time. Although he is not fully on board. He has some reservations."

"Such as?"

It was Evelyn's mother that spoke, "Evelyn made it seemed as if his mind was made up. Perhaps, we can call or meet with him put him at ease."

"No, Mother," the young woman quickly looked at Caesar before focusing on her parents, "there is no need and yes Caesar here is putting the finishing details on everything and once it's done we will sit down for dinner and discuss the great things this new experiment will do for all of us."

"Not to mention the new era of prosperity that will be ushered in." Caesar chimed in taking his que to further soothe the two elders of the Chad Coven. Despite them being Evelyn's parents, they weren't here on a social call.

They wanted to ensure he and Evelyn's union would prove beneficial for them. The two ruled over the Chadian council and were their coven's ambassadors. There was no way they would give their first born daughter to a foreign and second born son of alpha without a return on investment.

They were checking in and Caesar needed them to wait a little longer while the last few pieces fell into place.

After nearly two hours of reassurance Hamid and Zenab left.

He sighed undoing his tie as he headed for the kitchen. Evelyn was waiting a bottle of wine in her hand. She poured two glasses handing one to Caesar which he eagerly took.

Evelyn dismissed the maid for the evening and the two sat at the counter next to one another.

He sighed, "a head's up would have been nice."

"Sorry, I was ambushed. They were waiting for me when I came home, the housekeeper or rather former housekeeper let them in."

He scoffed.

"I take it the other tribes are just as restless?" He asked looking at her.

"Yes, the Nigerians are pushing to join the Spaniards and exclude the American covens altogether. They are growing agitated in some of the lower regions many of them are ready to come out of the shadows. Plus some of the poorer tribes are ready to finally benefit from their contributions and the protection they provide in the transportation of goods to the larger tribes." Evelyn stated taking a sip of wine.

He sighed rubbing his face. His shoulders slouched and she could tell he was tired they both were growing weary.

"You want to talk about all of this later?" Evelyn asked rubbing his shoulder. He nodded.

"Ok, what did you have to tell me?"

"Hmm?"

"You sounded like you had something to tell me when you came in earlier."

"Oh, I found a new lead. A relative of Madame Nikki. I will fly to Ohio tomorrow afternoon."

"We have dinner with your parents tomorrow."

"Damn, I forgot. You'll have to go without me. Can you make my excuses?"

She raised an eyebrow and he chuckled.

"You're right, the day after then."

GIANNA HAD BEEN ON a roll for the past week hitting two of the six leads she found all before lunch. The meetings didn't provide much of anything new and some of the details were a little grainy but she followed any and every lead.

She stopped for a late lunch her mind going back to the older woman she had spoken with before. It pertained to Madame Nikki the woman that had agreed to take her in and raise her when her birth mother abandoned her. Vaguely she remembered the cabin and the man that came looking for something, but her young mind couldn't grasp what was implied and had merrily watched in fascination. He was the first full wolf she had seen and even in her youth she recognized his authority. His raw power amazed her, and Gianna had a sinking feeling.

She stared at the picture in her phone. It was of the main antagonist in their little story. Maximillian DuBois. Her body froze as if she had an ah ha moment.

It was him.

Sweat appeared like bullets on her forehead. She remembered now. The memories moved like a freight train with no brakes, and she could only grip the table to brace herself as they slammed into her.

It was nearly midnight it had just rained. The light summer shower was a rarity and Nikki and Gianna danced earlier that evening in the heavy down pour. Both came in soaked and laughing. She had been there for nearly four months that day. Jan and her husband had taken her there and left. Jan had grown sick the cancer ravaging her already thin frame and a small child playing over oxygen tanks and pranking hospice care wasn't ideal.

Nikki being half wolf herself was the obvious choice to care for the odd little girl that had a proclivity for late nights and undercooked meat.

The two shared a bed and Gianna even now could feel the warm body snuggled against hers and the tight hold that Nikki always kept on her.

The man, the blonde came offering a piece of paper one that after he left Nikki had waved around holding up against the candlelight. Nikki had smiled down at her stating life was about to change for them both.

Unbeknownst to the Wiccan woman her predications were about to come true once again and not for the good.

Nikki sat up suddenly startling the child. Gianna only rubbed her eyes and rolled over ready to go back to sleep. She nearly screamed when she felt hands grab her small shoulders and pull her into a sitting position.

It was Nikki; the woman quickly placed a hand over her mouth.

"Someone's here. Listen."

Gianna tried to tune her hearing block out the noise of the crickets that sung their mating song trying desperately to recall all the woman who held her tight had taught her. She could only nod her eyes wide with fear. She didn't hear anything aside from the pounding of her heart.

"We have to move."

Nikki moved gracefully across the floor the child clutched to her chest. Gently, she placed Gianna on the floor in the kitchen, she could see the shadow now. They moved like mist outside the window and now she could hear the low growling of a predator.

"Close your eyes." Nikki hissed holding a jug of something clear.

She did as instructed and felt a hand hold her head down as she smelled the liquid. She shivered at the coldness. Gianna couldn't name it then but could now, it was ammonia. It was the same liquid that as an adult she refused to allow in her home. In this moment she understood why.

Next came the light scrapping of wood, it was the hidey hole underneath the rickety table. She kept her eyes closed as she felt her body being pushed down beneath it.

"Don't come out, no matter what happens." Nikki stated her mouth next to her and Gianna would hold on to the faint smell of sandalwood and cinnamon as full lips made contact with pink flesh. The last kiss from the woman she called mother.

It was like a flash, and she was back in the diner the thin waiter with a swoop bang and black nails looking down at her with a bored expression.

"We're out of mashed potatoes, do you want another side?"

The woman repeated her question in the same monotone voice that was the calling card of a woke generation that was over it. Whatever IT was.

"Umm, no. Never mind." She stood; Gianna was shaking. She fumbled around in her bag for her wallet pulling a small wad of twenties from it. Hurriedly, she pushed two Jacksons in the teen's hand and pulled the bag onto her shoulder.

She didn't breathe until she was on the sidewalk. There was more and she placed her hand on the side of the building to steady herself. She feared if she tried to walk to her car she wouldn't make it.

The large black wolf rose slowly onto two legs and its body contorted into that of a man. He was nude his frame large but fit. His dark yellow eyes bore into hers, but Nikki held her ground refusing to look away. Glistening skin nearly as dark as the shadow he cast.

"Tying up loose ends, Charles?"

He hesitated before answering.

"Something like that."

"Well, you better get to it you wouldn't want to upset Alpha Maximillian."

He took a deep breath.

"It should have been you, you know."

He hesitated letting the statement bounce around in his inner ear. The thought crossed his mind frequently. He could challenge exercise the same tactics his friend had there was still enough left in the vial for another dose.

"He will pay me back."

"You sure about that?"

Once again, he hesitated, he had two jobs. One of them was completed nearly two weeks prior, and three days ago, Maximillian delivered the fatal blow freeing them all from an entitled madman.

He needed to finish this final task and leave as quickly as possible. He had been there for over an hour. The majority of his time was spent working up the nerve to murder an innocent woman and child.

"I can make this quick and painless."

"Like you did for Samuel?"

He bristled clenching his jaw.

"Stop stalling, you don't have the strength nor the skill to stop me. Remember you're only half wolf."

She chuckled, "you and my father don't say. You and Maximillian are full blood wolves going back," she looked up dramatically as if deep in thought, "What at least two centuries and you had to resort to poison. A hollow victory indeed. What does that say about the two of you?"

Charles' hands shook and the guilt he wrestled with was making its presence known again. He blinked as if to refocus his eyes taking on their natural hue.

"It must end this way. Too many people know. I'm sorry," he whispered the apology and Nikki could sense the trepidation.

"Says who, your Alpha?"

"He's not my alpha," Charles hissed his eyes once again aglow. His shoulders squared the defeated stance from earlier gone.

"If you say so. You are another pawn in his game to power," she chuckled the tone rich and dark, "all of you are. Replacing one tyrant for another. I believe those were your words not mine."

The hairs on his arms stood up. It was if the woman could read his thoughts. He was beginning to doubt Maximilian, the plan, everything.

"Enough! Don't assume you know my thoughts witch! Now, where is the girl? I know she is here. I can smell the ammonia. Clever trick trying to disguise her scent. But I will find her."

During their conversation Nikki edged closer to the counter and the knife that lay on the sink. This did not go unnoticed by Charles, and he pounced just as she reached for the handle. The change happened at lightning speed just as jaws enclosed the woman's neck.

Nikki managed to grab the knife and brought the blade down into the side of his shoulder. Jaws still clamped around her throat he let out a muffled growl and sank his teeth deeper into her milky white flesh.

Gianna clenched her eye lids tighter and in a cruel act of fate her hearing tuned as she heard the gurgling of her caregiver. The struggled breathing made her nauseous and small hands covered her mouth to prevent her from screaming.

She had lain beneath the floor drenched in the cleaning solvent not moving until the first signs of daylight beamed through the worn floorboards.

What the little girl rose to find was the mangled body of the woman she had considered a mother. Slowly she approached the remains leaving small footprints in the congealed blood.

Gianna wasn't sure how she got back to her car, but she was behind the steering wheel of the Buick heading toward Camille's.

She reached for her phone it had chimed the sound echoing in the car. It was her contact with more information and more leads. Ginna knew it was Maximillian and Charles that were responsible for her mother's death.

Somehow, they would pay.

CAMILLE AND HER MOTHER were having brunch when her cell rang. She glanced at the screen and saw Gianna's name appear so did her mother.

Elizabeth sighed placing the teacup down with a thud.

"Are you still talking to that woman?"

Camille declined the call and sent a quick text letting Gianna know she would call her back once she was free. She made sure not to mention she was with their mother.

"That woman is your daughter, your eldest daughter." Camille rolled her eyes as she dropped the phone in her bag and placed it in the chair next to her.

Elizabeth smirked.

"My eldest daughter is earning her PhD at Cambridge and engaged to a nobleman, a not-so-distant cousin of the king, if I remember correctly. She's not here playing model and whoring herself out to a man that has shown he's more interested in a root canal than you."

The glow Elizabeth had when speaking about her second oldest daughter, Shannon, was gone replaced with an expression Camille could only compare to Salvador Dali's painting of melting clocks. The way her face fell, and the skin folded on itself you would have never guessed the woman was a frequent user of Botox.

Camille rolled her eyes.

"That is not my path, I am a model, and I wasn't whoring myself out to Armand."

"Keep telling yourself that dear."

Camille leaned forward to interject but was stopped when her mother held up her hand.

"Enough. You did redeem yourself with this real estate business of yours, however small," even offering a compliment the disdain still dripped from her voice like acrid honey, "it's still redemption. How's the market? Your father is looking to put Eagle's Peak up for sale although I am not sure why he would part with such a gorgeous property."

Camille sighed fingering the fork she looked down into her lap before she picked up the wine glass and took a long un-lady like sip.

"Well, just like you two isn't. Discard beautiful things that are no longer useful? Or convenient?"

Elizabeth regarded her daughter for a moment.

"What are getting at dear?"

"Nothing. The market is hot right now. People are looking for Southern vacation properties, I can get in touch with a few contacts. I'm sure I can have potential buyers by the end of the week."

Elizabeth smiled, happy with the change in conversation, "good. Let's discuss Shannon's wedding and what you will be wearing."

Camille reached for the bottle of wine on the table and slightly shook it. It was nearly empty, and she groaned. There wasn't enough wine to discuss her sister's upcoming wedding.

"Do we have to?" Camille sighed waving over the waiter.

"Yes, and since we are discussing weddings you should procure a dress for Caesar and Evelyn's upcoming nuptials. It will be a grand affair of course." Elizabeth stated with a sneer.

"Geez, Mom, what's that look about?"

"That could have been you, instead of wasting time with Armand you should have set your sights on the second," she held up her hands, "I know, I know. I just had to say it. Instead of marrying a foreigner Alpha Maximillian could have chosen within our own Coven."

"Allegiance. We are only as strong as the alliances we form."

"Yes but," Elizabeth took a sip of her tea, "did they have to get one so dark? All of the Coven talked about it for months."

Her mother looked down checking her phone, Camille took the moment to roll her eyes. Her mother's sentiments weren't surprising; she sighed and shook her head.

"Evelyn comes from a very old bloodline besides the world has changed and its time the Coven does as well."

Her mother scoffed, "too much change my dearest is not good. Especially rapid change."

GIANNA PRESSED THE call button and held her finger there until a disgruntled sounding young woman answered.

"Yes?"

"I'm here for Camille."

"Ms. Camille is not in." The woman's tone was clipped her voice heavy, and Gianna detected a French accent.

"It's her sister."

She was answered with a pause before the gate groaned her admittance as it slid to the side.

Camille skidded the Buick to a stop and nearly snatched the keys from the ignition. The front door opened, and a maid came to greet her. The woman looked confused as Gianna approached.

"You're not Ms. Shannon."

"Good eye sweety," Gianna through over her shoulder as she headed for the kitchen. She threw her bag on the counter and proceeded to go through the cabinets pulling out a wine glass before heading in the direction of the glass enclosed wine bottle rack and pulled out two bottles.

The maid followed looking frantic before the woman pulled out a phone and disappeared into the adjoining room. Gianna figured to call Camille which was a favor maybe the woman would rush home and Gianna could disclose all that she knew.

CAMILLE'S PHONE RANG this time it was her housekeeper and she smiled in relief.

Elizabeth was mid-sentence of her rant regarding the engagement of their alpha's youngest son with a woman of African descent when she stopped and stared at her younger daughter.

"Why are you smiling dear? Are you not upset? That should have been you, truly."

Camille shifted her gaze from the phone to her mother as she placed it to her ear.

"No, nobody wants Caesar he's weird and neurotic Mother and besides it's a new century get over it already, geez." Camille stood placing her purse on her shoulder.

"Where are you going?" Elizabeth looked affronted.

"I have a showing."

"Oh, how about I come with you. I'd like to see if that expensive UC Berkeley education paid off."

"Tell her to stay put; I'll be there shortly," Camille whispered.

She hung up and addressed her mother, "please mother you've spent that much on shopping trips. I have to go," she quickly hurried from the table before Elizabeth had a chance to collect her things and pay the bill.

"Next time," she through over her shoulder as she hurried out the gated outdoor eating area.

Twenty minutes had elapsed when Gianna heard the rapid clicks of heels and figured her sister was home.

Camille entered and stopped before she got to the counter, "Please tell me you have something?"

"I wouldn't be here if I didn't anything."

Gianna put out her cigarette and took a long sip of wine.

"How bad is it?" Camille asked noting that there were two bottles of wine on the counter one of them was clearly empty and figured the other wasn't too far behind.

She kicked off her heels.

"Francesca?" Camille called.

The French woman entered with her hands clasped in front. Her shoulders hunched, and Gianna could only speculate the young woman thought she was being fired.

"Take the day off. Let Kelsey know as well. You two can go home for the day."

"I'm sorry she," Francesca pointed at Gianna her eyes narrowed.

Camille held up her hand, "no it's fine. She's my sister and she is always welcomed here. Go, take the day." She patted the petite redhead on the shoulder.

It only took Camille five minutes to change clothes. She ensured the two of them were alone before she sat down with a third bottle of wine at the counter next to Gianna.

"I remember," Gianna began cuddling the wine glass to her chest an anchor for the stormy sea of emotions she was about to tread for the second time that day.

Camille listened connections were finally being made and she felt terrible. Armand, Amelia were simply pawns in a game that spanned at minimum two decades. Caesar wasn't trying to pull her into the fold as payment for services rendered it was part of his endgame; she was another pawn.

She wasn't sure what the man's endgame was but from what Gianna revealed and what she had gleamed a picture was being painted although more along the lines of a Basquiat the implications were clear.

Gianna was shaking at she finished. Quickly, she brought the glass to her lips and downed the maroon liquid.

Camille reached for Ginna's hand that rested on the counter, "I am so sorry that happened to you. I..." she trailed off. She was starting to get choked up and, in the moment, she was beginning to hate her mother and all those around her.

Hypocrites all of them.

"It's fine sweetheart." Her tone had taken on a sadness Camille would have thought was beyond the usually strong woman. As she spoke her gaze never left the granite.

"So, I just want to summarize make sure I'm hearing this shit correctly because if so," Camille let out a breath, "this is beyond treason this is a coup, in real life."

Gianna nodded finally looking at the younger woman, "yeah. Big shit, huge."

"Maximillian DuBois and Charles Anaheim conspired to kill Samuel Wiltshire, whom is the uncle of Cain Lewis. Cain and Armand were best friends until Danielle Fields is found dead in the apartment he shared with Armand. All clues point to Armand, so Daddy makes it go away and Armand is shipped off to Oxford. Cain leaves Dartmouth in shame disappearing completely until recently. Caesar wants Armand gone and wants me to help him do it."

"In a nutshell sis but yeah sounds about right."

Camille rubbed her face hard upending her left false eyelash.

"I have to get out of this. Caesar isn't going to let anyone leave. He needs Cain to get rid of Armand his hands are clean and once he takes over, he hunts down Cain for killing his brother. He comes out the hero." Camille was thinking aloud speaking to herself more than to Gianna.

The other watched smirking glad that her sister understood.

Laying Claim

Armand arranged the details based on the information Tina gleamed during her reconnaissance mission of Amelia. This would be the young heir's first and most important attempt to woo the not so easily impressed young woman.

The usual shallow conversation with the vapid women looking to score with the alpha's son never required much beyond his attention. Once his primal needs were sated he moved on.

He gave the thirty something year old the green light to use all of her former Naval training. Once the woman's likes and dislikes were in hand Armand had agonized over the perfect date since asking her out three days prior.

His assistant booked out the entire restaurant. It was a new age upscale Asian place that opened a few months ago. For her he had pulled out all the stops.

AMELIA BARELY HAD ANY privacy as they all stood at the threshold to her room.

Her mother fawned over her, her brothers teased, and aunts stood against the wall watching. Aunt Nancy's eyes judgmental the lids to those round orbs squinted slightly. Aunt Stella stood a slight smirk on her face as she approached sliding a small vial into her right hand.

"Two dabs on each side of the neck," was whispered against her ear causing Amelia to chuckle.

Diane quickly shooed Stella away hogging Amelia from the others. She managed to get them out her father only nodding at her as he ushered her mother from the room. The others soon followed, and she finished dressing.

ARMAND LEFT THE OFFICE early going back to his apartment to dress for his date. Normally, he would have had his assistant call a maid service to give the usually spotless penthouse a once over in preparation for a sexual tryst but given he wanted to make a good impression he didn't bother.

Not to mention the five foot seven amber skinned Amelia was different, he was in no rush to bring her there and when he did the moment would be nothing short of perfect.

He paused in front of the floor length mirror. He searched for any signs he had lost his mind. The care in which he planned this date was uncharacteristic of him. Before he could ponder further his phone chimed alerting him a text had come through.

It was Hera with a message encouraging him not to 'fuck it up'. He rolled his eyes as he placed the phone in the pocket of his blazer. He checked his watch noting he needed to get on the interstate and head to Amelia's.

He arrived at the large estate fifteen minutes before the time he said he'd pick her up. He knocked twice before the door opened revealing an older woman.

Armand cleared his throat, "Good Evening, I'm here for..."

"I know why you're here," Nancy hissed as she stepped back opening the door wider to allow him in, "you're here for my niece, another notch in your belt Prince Armand," she spat out the later and the title he hated.

"Enough," Diane hissed as she approached her eyes cold. Nancy's gaze remained on Armand as his shifted to Diane.

"Please accept my apologies and disregard my aunt. This way. Amelia will be down shortly," Diane led him into the sitting room casting a hard glance at Nancy as she and Armand passed.

Nancy watched the pair her right eye slightly aglow the hair on her arms were rigid. The soft hairs had grown as hard as needles.

Armand reflexively tensed as he sensed the older woman's change in energy. If Diane felt it he couldn't tell as she continued chatting asking after his mother.

"She's well. Fawning over me unfortunately and Mrs. Anaheim it's alright, I understand your aunt is from a different time. Before the formation of the coven and all that we know today."

Diane smiled guiding him to a couch, "I'll be back and call me Diane please." She left the room hurriedly nearly jogging out.

Liam entered a Cheshire grin on his face Mason was more serious his long lanky form shrouded in black with neon green vans on his feet. Both boys came and sat one on each side of him. Armand could only drop his head to hide his smile.

He and Caesar put on a similar performance when suitors came calling for their baby sister. Both unlike the two sheltered boys beside him, Armand and Caesar did the menacing act naturally. Armand had killed before he wasn't sure about his brother, but he knew him well enough to know his younger sibling wasn't above the deed.

Armand was sure the two young men had probably never so much as growled at another wolf. But he would play along simply for amusement.

"Armand," Mason drawled as he casually placed an arm around his shoulder pulling him close.

Liam stayed silent the side shave cut with his dreads partially obscuring his right eye made him look more comical than edgy.

"What are your intentions?" Liam asked in a harsh whisper. He seemed scared but Armand noted he was doing a good job of disguising it.

He angled his body slightly, "I assure you my intentions are pure. I give you my word. I will do no harm to your sister."

Liam stared at him lips forming into a thin line, "you better do right by her." Armand looked down he felt a slight poke in his chest and noted Liam had a slim index finger pointed in the middle of his sternum.

"See," Mason cut in giving Armand's should a squeeze and simultaneously pulling him causing him to lean awkwardly to the side, "what my little bro is trying to say is we care about our big sis you know, and we want to know that the dude she's out with has the right things in mind. Amelia is smart special and although you may be the future alpha and what not, if you hurt our sister then," Mason looked around dramatically his gaze fell back on Armand, "then we have to hurt you, got it?"

Armand focused staring straight ahead he wanted to bellow out in laughter and fought hard to hold it in so he simply nodded until he could speak.

"I have a sister as well, so I understand."

Mason moved his hand to his back and gave him two hard pats, "good, good."

The two boys rose towering over his sitting frame. The clacking of approaching heels could be heard and the two looked at one another before hurrying out the opposite door.

Just as Amelia and Diane entered Armand rose. He stopped breathing when his eyes landed on Amelia.

The two stared at each other.

Diane smiled and after a minute of silence cleared her throat causing the two to jump slightly.

"You two should get going."

"Yes, of course," he turned his attention back to Amelia, "you look beautiful, amazing." He clamped his mouth shut in fear that he would start rambling. He didn't want to make things awkward.

ARMAND BLABBED ON THE drive to the restaurant about his role in the company and his adventures in Spain. He was sure to keep the women that flowed in and out of his bed out of the story.

Armand glimpsed down at his watch the ride was taking longer than expected. He wiped his hands on his thigh, his palms had grown sweaty when he realized they were nearly there. He had given Tina strict instructions to carry out. Although he had never doubted the woman's ability to deliver, he hoped she would be pleased.

The driver pulled in front and the attendant rushed to open Armand's door. He stepped out the cool arrogance was back as he glided around the car to Amelia's side and opened the door. He extended a hand which she eagerly took.

Amelia had taken the few seconds it took for him to walk around to her side of the car to lightly tap her palms against the beaded black dress she wore. With the hair and the fresh manicure not to mention the slight V of the dress she felt exposed.

She took a deep breath releasing it as she stepped out her gaze firmly on her feet and the stilettos her mother had surprised her with last minute. Amelia gasped as his large hand made contact with her lower back the touch, although appropriate and friendly, set her skin ablaze.

Armand felt the sharp intake of breath and it set off one of his own. He had to suppress the urge to pull her against him and shred the dress that clung to her body.

"I don't remember *The Lily* having valet." She whispered smiling and looking around.

"For us it does." He winked and she chuckled.

Armand could have sworn it was the sweetest sound he'd ever heard.

They entered to find the host waiting along with his assistant Tina. Armand took a moment to give the decor and changes he requested a once over. He was satisfied and gave Tina a slight nod which she returned before bidding the couple good night.

The hostess quickly showed them to a secluded area although they were the only diners of the evening Armand still wanted privacy and this part of the restaurant offered the accommodation.

The waitress quickly handed them a menu and took their drink orders. Amelia kept it simple ordering a wine.

They sat in silence their eyes locked briefly before Amelia quickly averted her gaze. The heat and passion she saw in them would overtake her. His gaze was hypnotic, and she found it difficult to look away.

Something stirred in his groin and reflexively crossed his leg over his thigh. He didn't want her to see him as a man that simply wanted to bed her. He cared what she thought and for once that didn't make him uncomfortable like it had previously.

Amelia resisted the urge to bite at the manicure and instead fidgeted beneath the table. She was unsure of herself and what to say.

The waitress brought out appetizers carefully placing the dishes in front of them. She waited until given a nod of approval from Armand before bowing and leaving the two.

Amelia began, "everything is beautiful."

She stared down at her plate.

"Is the food not to your liking?" He was about to call for the server when she spoke.

"No, the food is perfect. It's just..." she trailed off slightly embarrassed.

"This is my first real date. I don't get asked out often. I'm sorry if I'm...boring. I'm sure you've been out with more interesting women."

She looked down and Armand could sense her embarrassment and something else. It was faint and to a casual observer it would have been missed but he saw it. Shame. He had the urge the need to reassure her.

He placed his hand on the table. Sensing his movement, she looked up and slowly placed her hand in his. Normally she would have scoffed at the idea of seeking male comfort. But his presence nullified whatever bit of feminism that made up her ideology.

"Amelia, you shouldn't be ashamed nor feel embarrassed. This is my first date as well."

She rolled her eyes playfully blushing slightly.

"I highly doubt it." Playfully she rolled her eyes as she started to pull her hand away. He tightened his hold causing her breath to hitch.

"No, I'm serious I wouldn't lie to you. I've never done this for anyone. Only you." His eyes had gone pitch black and she couldn't help becoming mesmerized by their intensity for a second time. She swallowed hard her breathing was uneven as she crossed her legs. The young woman mentally shook herself to clear her head.

"I believe you." She sighed needing to pull her hand away. The dress was becoming uncomfortable, and she had a desire to touch his face. She needed this man to want her as much as she wanted him.

She abruptly stood jerking her hand away.

"Sorry, I need to use the restroom." She breathed out and turned not waiting for a response and headed toward the back of the restaurant.

Armand took in a sharp breath and loosened his tie. It took all the restraint he could muster not to take her on the table. Her desire was just as strong as his making the evening thus far very difficult for his self-control.

He reached for the glass of cognac but thought better of the decision to mix hard liquor and his yearning for the virgin he had to share a car with, instead he pushed it back picking up the glass of sparkling water.

This was only the first half of their date, and he needed a clear head.

Amelia stared at her reflection, she was horny painful and frightfully so and she dug in her clutch for her phone. Her thumb hovered above Lacie's number, but she simply pressed the button causing the screen to go black. Her mind went to dial her mother, but her advice would be the same as Amber's although less vulgar.

'You are a grown ass woman sleep with the man if you like.' Lacie's words echoed in her mind.

She sighed pulling at the hem of the dress. Amelia whispered an affirmation and headed back to the table.

"Sorry. I didn't mean to bale on you, I just needed a moment."

"I understand. I did as well."

"What do you like?" Amelia asked picking up her chopsticks.

"What do you mean Ms. Anaheim? You haven't been raised to know my every desire?" He wore a smirk, and he watched the array of emotions flutter across her face.

She laughed when she realized he was merely teasing.

"Sorry to disappoint Mr. DuBois but you are not the center of every young female wolf's world."

Armand mockingly clutched his chest.

"No? Really?"

"Nope, not even a little."

NEXT WAS A PRIVATE tour of the not yet available to the public exhibit. Armand's heart leapt at the way her eyes lit up changing color from a smoky grey to a deep green.

The two held hands and Armand almost felt like he was in fairy tale. The evening wrapped up with the pair sitting in a secluded area of a park gazing up at the moon. Selene hung low and large, and the two young wolves felt the pull of her fullness.

Amelia wanted Armand that she was sure of surer than the need to breath.

She rose onto her knees. He rose to his as well the dessert forgotten between them.

"Armand," she whispered his naming heightening the longing he had for her all night.

He answered by pulling her closer and into a kiss. She placed her arms around his neck pulling him closer. With her breasts against his chest he grew hard. Amelia felt his manhood through the thin fabric of the dress.

On instinct he placed his hand between her legs resting on her inner thigh she moaned, and Armand broke the kiss.

"We shouldn't. We need to stop."

She looked confused thinking his hesitation was a rejection of her. "Why?"

"Because if we keep going, I won't be able to stop. I'm at the point I'm in need of you. I can't stop."

Her face relaxed and the excitement returned. What if I don't want you to stop?"

She asked watching him searching for any micro signs.

"This isn't a game for me Amelia. I want you more than anything I've wanted in my life. I want you to be my mate. If you say yes, I will have no other. Do you consent to be my mate?"

Her jaw slackened causing her mouth fall slightly agape. The breath she drew in was shaky. Mates were something she had read about and knew of no one that experienced such a connection. Not even her parents.

Amelia responded without giving his question further thought.

"Yes. I consent."

His lips fell upon hers and he guided them down onto the blanket her small frame nestled underneath his. He covered her gently tearing the dress in half. Amelia did the same although she fumbled out of nervousness but soon conquered the emotion and allowed nature to overtake any doubt.

When he entered her, Amelia's body took over and she arched into him. Armand nearly howled as he sank into her tight heat. She was exquisite and he knew he would kill for her.

They lay exhausted as Amelia took note of how her body felt after having sex for the first time. She smiled thinking she would have a story to tell Lacie tomorrow morning.

"I should get you home." Armand didn't bother to move as his arm tightened around her.

"What if I don't want to go home?"

She looked up at him.

He smiled down at her.

"Ok."

They dressed Amelia doing her best to salvage the dress as Armand placed his jacket around her and the two walked with their arms around one another to the SUV.

They arrived at his apartment and Armand had barely shut the door when Amelia began to pull at his shirt ripping the button down. He picked her up and she wrapped her legs around his middle.

He walked them to his bedroom and gently placed her in the middle of the bed. He stepped back looking down at her.

Amelia shuddered his face had darken with lust as he slid down his trousers. She bit her bottom lip as she watched his manhood rise the tip up near his belly button. Armand lowered himself to his knees in supplication Amelia could only look on in astonishment her eyes aglow she had never given herself to a man nor even thought about it; the idea of spinsterhood was more palatable than submission.

She leaned back spreading her thighs sighing and Armand slowly crawled from the floor between them.

For the second time that evening they joined they were nearing a climax and Armand brought his canines down on her trapezius growling as he did so. She moaned her pleasure as the hairs on her arms stood.

Once they came down from the high of their sexual encounter, she slowly brought her hand up to her neck feeling the two indentations.

He stroked the side of her face, "it's official. You're my mate."

SHE GROANED THE SORENESS in her crotch was no contender for that in her neck. Naturally curious of their kind she had read and studied what to expect when being claimed by a male as a mate. What she envisioned had been a fairy tale. Although pleasurable, there weren't any fireworks nor did the Earth stop spinning but she did feel lighter.

She rose from the bed heading naked to the bathroom each movement, no matter how mundane, had purpose.

Armand woke with her movement. He felt that soreness down below and wondered did he need to comfort her although he wasn't sure how. She was his now. That meant a soul tie. Hearing about the act of Laying Claim he thought it would be more ritualistic maybe last night had been he had never paid much attention during the tutoring sessions to notice any difference.

Truthfully, he didn't care about the formalities. He had found what he needed, and he wouldn't let her go. He sighed; he would have to explain to her parents especially her father as well ask her for her hand in marriage.

Amelia returned to bed she couldn't help but smile, Armand wore the same expression he had shortly before he had laid claim and her body responded. The soreness and the hunger pains forgotten as they made love.

It was nearly four hours later when she found herself in the passenger seat and on the way home. Nervousness had finally set in beating out the excitement she had initially felt. She would have to explain this to her mother, and she wasn't sure how her parents would feel.

He parked out front and went around to open her door. Armand helped her out staring up at the large home. It appeared ominous and Armand's palms felt clammy, but he was dead set on letting them know his intentions.

Amelia went to put her key into the lock and gasped when the door opened revealing her Aunt Nancy the woman wore a wild expression. She sniffed lightly before the light gray irises darkened. The hiss morphed into a low growl.

"He has you too."

Nancy stepped forward, "you murderer! Just like your father claiming and taking what isn't yours!" she shouted addressing Armand. He stood watching his expression blank.

Diane came rushing forward her hand on her mid-section as she held together her robe.

"What in the world? Nancy!"

She lightly pushed the woman that had been blocking the entrance aside and stood looking at her daughter and Armand.

She looked them over before her eyes went wide at the mark on the side of Amelia's neck. Diane gasped bringing her hand up to cover her mouth.

"Get in here you two, now!" Diane reached for them pulling them over the threshold and pulling them down a long hall into the first-floor library.

"Mom?" Amelia began but Diane quickly held up her index finger.

"No, I have to get your father." She turned to leave but spun on her heels and pulled Armand and Amelia into a hug.

"I've been waiting for this day," she sighed sniffling she released them and stepped back, "I'll get your father."

She moved quickly leaving before Amelia could speak.

"That went better than expected," Armand turned to Amelia a slight smile on his face. She returned the smile reaching for his hand. She had the urge to touch him and from the way his breath hitched, and his eyes darken he had more on his mind than the chaste hand holding.

Charles stopped a few feet from the door.

Diane had given him the news and he wasn't sure why dread had settled into his muscles causing them to ache. He sighed; this should have been welcomed news, but willowy dark-skinned man somehow felt he had cheated his daughter out of something. He felt like a used oil towel at his father's old auto shop in Selma.

He sighed, Maximillian owed him this and he would claim the reward for his misdeed. Charles entered to find the two staring at each other, and he coughed lightly. They both looked at him startled, Amelia cider-colored cheeks flushing a deep maroon. Armand stood stoic unsure of how to proceed.

"Amelia please join your mother I need to talk to Armand."

Amelia looked over at her new found love a little scared but he gave her hand a firm squeeze and their fingers parted, and she walked into her mother's outstretched arm. Diane gave her husband one final look as they left leaving the two men to talk.

Charles sighed, "as I understand, you have laid claim."

"Yes, I have." Armand straighten holding the older man's gaze.

The patriarch simply nodded.

"Very well then," he paused regarding his son's best friend, "you know our ways, so I won't ask your intentions. You do understand what you have done?"

Armand nodded, "of course. I have made my decision. I..." he trailed off unsure if he wanted to be so vulnerable with this man, "I am in love with your daughter. She's all I think about. She's all I have thought about since I returned home and saw her."

Armand kneeled his gaze on the floor, "I am asking for permission to marry Amelia and for you to accept my right of claim on your daughter as my mate."

A long silence permeated the air and although Armand couldn't see it, the man before him wore a pained expression.

"Yes, to both."

Armand let out a breath and slowly stood.

"You won't regret this. Amelia will be well taken care of."

"I know she will and I better not."

DIANE PACED NERVOUSLY around her eldest. She never though this day would come and now she was scared and giddy. Her long locs bounced against her back each time, she made a sharp turn Diane's gaze never leaving Amelia.

"I'm sorry," she whispered.

Diane stopped her eyes wide as she rushed toward her.

"No, don't be sorry. This is great. When your father accepts Armand's right of claim, he better accept, you are pretty much Armand's bride no ceremony needed. Although the council will want to make it official no doubt Maximillian as he will be the alpha." She clapped and reached out stroking Amelia's face.

"Wow, you pulled a future alpha."

Diane was smiling her eyes bright.

Amelia looked away she had been so caught up in the rapture of love that she didn't think of being Armand's mate would entail. She would voice her opinion aloud, but she was terrified, and she thought of how she could end this new found romance with Armand before it went further.

"What if I rescind?" she asked stepping back and out of mother's grasp.

"And ruin all of this family's hard work?"

"You mean scheming and plotting behind my back. Aunt Nancy told me enough," Amelia whispered unsure of why she had placed her aunt on the spot.

"All lies. Lies of an old woman that didn't act to utilize her youth and beauty wasting it on a no-good human for what? To end up a maid. I am the only one that would take her in and she's old and bitter. Now that she is beyond her prime, she wants to fuck up everybody else's chances. She did the same thing with me when it came to your father. Like I would pass up marrying into one of the founding families of a coven. I see she's trying to sink her claws into you!"

Amelia ignored her, "who are the Wiltshire's? What happened to them?"

Diane paused watching her daughter curious as to what her aunt had been telling Amelia about the past. A tinge of panic ran through her and she breath deep.

"This is the greatest day of your life, and you are worried about the insane ramblings of a dried up hag?" Diane hissed.

"Don't call her that."

"It's true, darling," she approached Amelia grabbing her by the arms and rubbing them, "what's really wrong?"

She sighed, "I guess I am just nervous. I really love him. Do you think he feels the same?" Amelia decided to deflect. Her mother was getting nervous, and she could smell her rising fear.

"Of course." She pointed to the bruising and marks on her neck, "he wouldn't have done that if he didn't."

"You sure?"

"Very."

Diane cupped her daughter's face and stroked her cheeks with her thumbs.

"Then bask in this moment. He's yours just as much as you are his. Let the past be." She smiled and pulled Amelia into a hug.

DIANE FOUND NANCY IN the kitchen preparing dinner. The matriarch had given her sons Liam and Mason strict instructions to keep their sister out for a few hours while she talked to her great aunt.

"What have you been telling Amelia?"

Nancy continued with her task humming as she kneaded the dough for the pie.

"You old bitch you better say something," Diane hissed.

The old woman stopped looking up at her a smirk gracing her lips. The grey and hazy eye on her the brown one looking through her.

"I'm sorry, forgive me, but you have no right to meddle." Diane spoke her hands in the air in surrender. She gripped the edge of the counter using it as support as she leaned forward.

"You have no idea how far or how deep this goes. Armand has claimed Amelia, my daughter okay. My little brown baby to be his mate and she will be his wife. Your great niece. She will head this Coven by his side. Do you know how huge that is? Do you know what this means for all of us?" Her eyes were large as she fought to convey the severity of the implication.

"So. You would give your daughter to a family of frauds and murderers for what? A statement? I thought better of you Diane. But," she resumed kneading, "then you married that filth Charles after all he has done." She hissed as she delicately placed the dough in the pan using her calloused fingertips to shape the edges.

"It doesn't matter," she sighed, "I don't know why I thought you would understand. I want you out. Daniel will take you back to Centreville in the morning. Pack your things make your excuses and at first light I want you gone. I've already made arrangements you won't have to worry about money."

She crossed her arms, "you've crossed one too many lines. I can tolerate it no longer."

Nancy stopped her hands at her sides.

"Fine. I will do as you wish."

Diane nodded. "Thank you for understanding. I'm sorry it has to be this way."

Nancy placed her pie in the oven and turned to face her niece "no you're not. You know I don't have any love for Charles. I've always thought you made a mistake. Being with a man that didn't claim you. You were always a power hungry woman it seems you simply met your match. I wish you the best and I hope Amelia doesn't get entangled in the snares."

Before Diane could respond the woman was rounding the corner.

DINNER HAD BEEN A FEAST to rival any upcoming royal engagement.

Diane invited several relatives over to mark the occasion. Amelia had barely gotten a moment to eat in peace before she gave up and made her excuses as she pushed away from the table. The praise and questions felt out of place. The advice and the numerous vials Aunt Stella had placed in the pockets of her overalls felt just as heavy as the pressure of being in a bubble felt.

She found solace in the basement. She was still nervous and thinking on what little options she had left. She could do it later tonight. Rescind his claim. It would hurt no doubt both parties would be devastated possibly growing sick from the rejection. After a few weeks they would be fine, and he would move on to another.

"Lost in thought?"

Her head snapped up and she smiled at her aunt.

"Why weren't you at dinner? Mom practically invited everyone. "

"You mother doesn't want me there. She's always been one that couldn't handle the truth no matter who told it to her." she sighed. "She's not like you. Thinking of rescinding Armand's claim?"

She was always astonished at the old woman's ability to know what was going without you having to say a word. It was something she wished it was an ability her mother possessed. It would make talking to her easier.

"Yes. But now I don't know if I can live without him. Things have changed. I want to be with him all the time. I won't change my mind he'd die and so would I."

Nancy smirked.

"You two wouldn't die, fall ill for a while, yes but Death isn't ready for you two. Not yet. I wasn't fully honest with you that night. I told you some things but not all."

She motioned for her to sit on the chair, the grey haired woman took the seat opposite her.

"Your father is not the man he presents himself to be. Nor is Armand's but I can't help but hate the young man just the same. That family has murdered more wolves than what should have been allowable. But the Coven was just forming, and Samuel had just been challenged and killed."

Amelia looked away before focusing on Nancy, "sometime that happens. The first few years of the Coven were dangerous, but everything is when it is new. Clearly that's not the case now." She raised and lowered her shoulders in defeat clearly grasping at an explanation for the violence that was the bedrock of all their foundation.

Nancy chuckled, "don't let Armand's affection blind you to his true nature. You know he killed a girl. Danielle Fields."

She hissed standing, "I don't believe it."

Nancy slowly reached for her hand, "sit child. There were many things I didn't say but since I will no longer be here I will say them now for your sake."

Amelia slowly sat. She was overcome with dread causing the room to feel claustrophobic and hot.

"Where should I begin?" Nancy whispered to herself as she sat her eyes closed her hand still holding onto her great niece's.

"The beginning would be nice. Start there."

Her eyes fluttered open as a slight smile appeared on her face. The cloudy eye had almost grown black matching the iris of the other.

"Yes, I'll start there."

Unlike before the elder did not hold back and told the young woman everything leaving Amelia panicked as she went upstairs to her room.

She locked the door.

In the days and nights they had spent together Armand failed to mention any of this especially, Danielle. She fell onto her bed; the truth was she didn't know much about him aside from what everyone else knew. She brought her hand up to her forehead slapping her palm against the bone several times before she started to sob.

How could she let a man she barely knew lay claim to her body and dictate her future.

Armand

His assistant had stood over him for a solid two minutes. Gently she cleared her throat capturing his attention causing him to shift his gaze from the window. He gestured for her to come forward leaving his hand outstretched to receive the envelope.

"Is this what I asked for earlier?"

"No sir, still waiting on my contact, but this came this morning by courier. No name or return address. It was brought up by reception I wasn't sure whether to accept it but I had security scan it. Nothing nefarious." She stated waiting partially out of curiosity as well as for dismissal.

"That's all Tina, thank you."

"Yes sir," she nodded turning and leaving her boss alone.

He held the envelope curious as to who would send him this as his mind went to Amelia and the night before. He smiled and he became unnaturally hot as he thought of her. It was her first time and he felt deeply honored she had consented to share with him something so precious.

He opened the envelope half preoccupied with an email that had come through from one of his companies on the West coast before he brought his gaze to rest on the photo in his hand.

It was him and Amelia the young woman's head thrown back in passion. His face buried between her thighs as he lapped at her core. Across the photo written in black marker was *Danielle, a life for a life* with an 'X' over Amelia's face.

He abruptly stood knocking over his chair.

He shouted for Tina; she was within the doorway in seconds looking around before she locked eyes with Armand.

"Who brought this?"

"I am not sure sir; it was delivered by courier. No name, no address. It was left downstairs with reception."

He stared at the photo.

"Is there something wrong? Should I call security?"

He hesitated, "no, that's all Tina, thank you. Hold my calls and clear my schedule, something has come up. I have to go."

"Yes sir," she left to do as instructed and Armand grabbed his phone.

He rushed from his office and toward the stairs. He wouldn't bother with the slow descent in the metal box from the twenty eighth floor. At the moment his only concern was getting to Amelia he feared she may be in danger.

He dialed her number. After several rings it went to voice mail, so he tried again as he reached the parking deck. He was near his car and on the third call she answered. He breathed a sigh of relief stopping to place his hand over his heart.

"Hello, sorry I didn't answer right away. But I saw your calls is everything alright?" her voice had taken on a hint of concern.

He was silent trying to wrangle in his emotions.

"Armand?"

"Yes, I am here. Yes, everything is fine. I just needed to hear your voice. I am sorry to call you in the middle of the day."

"No, don't apologize I'm glad you called," her voice was soft, she missed him.

Her voice trailed off and Armand slowly climbed into the driver's seat of his car the phone still pressed to his ear. He wanted to say so many things but wasn't sure how to begin.

He checked his watch.

"Where are you? We can do lunch; I would love to see you. I need to see you," he whispered his voice husky and rough similar to the night before in the park.

"I am at Clybourne's Books, it's a small coffee shop about four blocks over. My meeting should wrap up in a few."

Armand was about to speak when a deep voice cut in.

"Is everything okay Amelia?"

He bristled at the familiar baritone and gripped the wheel. He had confirmation shortly after Amelia whispered a quick 'hold on a sec.'

"Yes, Mr. Lewis."

"Please, call me Cain. We've talked for nearly three hours we are pretty much friends if not we're definitely on first names bases." They both laughed and Armand became angry.

"I have to go my love."

She hung up before he could respond. Armand started the engine and quickly put the car in reverse backing out of the space and racing out of the parking deck.

He arrived to find Amelia and Cain on the sidewalk just having finished their meeting. Cain pulled Amelia into an embrace the man holding her longer and closer than necessary.

Armand had gotten out and approached them. He cleared his throat. Cain watched Armand approach a slight smirk on his lips. He slowly pulled away from the woman smiling down at her.

"I look forward to working with you." He gave her shoulder a slight squeeze before casting a final glance at his former friend. Cain departed without a second glance at Armanda.

"Who was that?" Armand asked curious to how much Cain had revealed to Amelia.

"Cain Lewis. I met him at the gala, and we exchanged numbers. He likes what I am doing with girls from low income families. He wants to get involved start something similar for orphaned teen boys."

She shrugged.

"You're not jealous, are you?" she asked playfully wrapping her arms around his mid-section. He placed his arm around her possessively as he watched Cain disappear around the corner.

"He's trouble."

"You know him?"

He paused not sure how to respond before he chose to omit the truth for now.

"No, just a feeling."

Amelia watched Armand for a moment before she shifted her gaze down the block in the direction Cain had walked.

"Hmm, I wonder how he got that scar." She whispered.

Armand stiffened, it did not go unnoticed, and she made a mental note to speak with her Aunt Stella once she was back home. Maybe the older woman could shed light on parts her Aunt Nancy left out.

Tonight, would be a prime opportunity most of the family wouldn't be home.

"Who knows? Lunch?" he looked down at her smiling.

"Sure."

He placed a kiss on her forehead as he led her to the car. Cain was forgotten temporarily but he made note to address him face to face soon.

HE ROSE EARLY THAT morning the scent of her mingled with his own. Showering was a task he enjoyed but this morning it was bittersweet as the water rolled down his skin taking with it the night they had enjoyed together.

He entered the office on a high even the traffic hadn't shifted his mood, and he greeted the receptionist with a smile and a cheery hello. This caused the woman to pause and do a double take making sure it was the owner and not an imposter.

He arrived to find a small package on his desk and a dark purple note card. Placing his briefcase and coffee down he picked it up turning it over.

He chuckled tossing it next to the coffee and Armand held the small vial up to the light. The substance it contained was dark black and he gave it a slight shake.

"Tina!"

The woman came charging in her notepad at the ready as she stood waiting for her marching orders.

"This package, where did it come from and when?"

"It was a delivery from a Madame Nikki the note attached said 'Because of your Father' we ran it through the scan nothing out of the ordinary."

He held the vial toward her. She gasped and moved forward to get a better look.

"Should I have Dean run it in the lab?"

He chuckled, "no, not for jello."

She looked at him surprised, "how..." she trailed off and smiled as Armand tapped his nose.

"I know."

"My apologies sir, sometimes I forget."

"No problem, how is the rest of my day looking?"

"You have a budget review at one thirty and a call with your father at four. Shall I cancel?"

"Ah no, that's perfect. Maybe he'll know something about this," he gestured to the vial he had placed next to a voided check for a hundred grand. The check had been left on the windshield of his car yesterday afternoon.

"Of course, sir, anything else."

"No, thank you, Tina."

She nodded before turning on her heel and disappearing beyond the glass doors.

HE SAT THROUGH THE budget meeting on edge his leg bouncing; he was anxious. Occasionally his eyes would land on the clock and stay there watching the hands move at an agonizing pace.

Caesar watched his brother during the meeting he was thinking and decided it was time to up the ante. He had given his brother one name- Madame Nikki. The half breed had left behind a small journal underneath a floorboard in the bedroom. It was a diary of some sort spanning back years and giving her history. She was the illegitimate daughter of councilman Daniel Spencer. From Nikki's account her mother grew tired of her position as the mistress and left but not before conceiving a half wolf child. She died giving birth the following spring.

But there was more, the weather beaten notebook contained her encounter with their father and even mentioned Charles. Caesar scanned copies and prepared two packages one for his father and brother.

Caesar tisked as he continued to watch his brother a smile spreading across his face like hot butter. He would need to move faster. His next meeting would be with Cain. He wanted to know where the man's head was and if an alliance could be formed.

The meeting ending the same as the others with the speaker nervously waiting feedback from the DuBois brothers. Caesar made his remarks keeping them short Armand simply waved his hand in dismissal before rising from the chair and leaving the room.

It was six minutes to the four.

Their conversation began it was the usual business chatter and he got the rare compliment from his father.

"Caesar said you're doing well."

Armand rolled his eyes annoyed; he would have a word with his young brother. He did not like being observed and reported on. The eldest DuBois would have said as much but his father was uncharacteristically jovial.

He chose to voice his displeasure another time.

"I was thinking," Maximillian began," how about we all have dinner, you, Caesar, and Hera, tomorrow night."

Armand knew it was rare that his father made a request, but it would be better for him to accept.

"I'll be there, Father before you go have you heard of someone named Madame Nikki?" Armand paused waiting for a response; he was met with silence. Quickly he checked his desk phone to ensure the call hadn't disconnected prematurely.

"Father?"

"No."

The answer was short clipped and although he couldn't see the man, he sensed the change in his father.

"Why do you ask?"

Armand hesitated unsure of whether to mention the package and the vial. He chose to sit on the information for now until he had more.

"Nothing, an old piece of cardstock or something. The name just sounded odd."

Maximillian sighed into the phone.

"Okay, son. See you at dinner."

The call ended and Armand glanced at the clock it was nearly six. He pressed the call button and dismissed Tina for the evening.

He grabbed the slip of paper from his desk that contained coordinates. When going through the land development records, he noticed an address that appeared to have no known purpose. From Google maps he could tell the location was remote and wondered why his father would have purchased a piece of property and left it untouched.

He put the coordinates into this phone and began the hour-long drive.

ARMAND ARRIVED AT A dilapidated cabin. He could tell it once held a rustic elegance, but time had taken its beauty and charm leaving only the scenic grace of the area.

He shut off the motor and exited the car quietly closing the door. An unsettling feeling weighed him down; although he could sense he was alone he remained alert.

Armand walked the few feet to the cabin and pushed open the door. It creaked as if it had a secret to tell. The floorboards protested under his weight and Armand sighed. Of all the things he could do on a Friday night this was the less entertaining of the choices.

The eldest DuBois walked the entire cabin circling back to the small kitchen. He stooped fingering a large dark spot. The wood had been rubbed smooth, very distinct from the other areas of the house.

He took a deep breath any scents that the decay didn't mask would have been washed away due to the weather. Armand left the items as well as the cabin forgotten as the young brown beauty occupied his mind.

DINNER WAS AN ILLUSTRIOUS affair. Hemesh pulled out all the stops thankful to the point of giddiness that all of her children were home and at her dinner table.

Hera making the rare appearance from yoga and her studies sat a slight smirk on her face. Her coal hair glistening in the overhead light of the large dining room. She was the replica of their Aunt Samira, but she had taken on a fairer completion her hue just slightly darker than their father's.

Caesar was even the center of attention keeping the conversation flowing. The laughter passed around the table like a tidal wave and

Armand found himself going along adding bits when appropriate biding his time for the questions he wanted to ask.

After the staff had placed the next course, he cleared his throat breaking the clatter of forks against the bone China.

"Father?"

"Yes, Armand?" Maximillian watched him expectantly a rare smile gracing his lips.

"I ran across something curious a piece of property, a small cabin."

The smile waned, "oh," was all he uttered picking up his wine glass.

"It's an old, dilapidated cabin."

"Oh," Maximillian nodded, "yes an old buy up from the late eighties or early '91. I can't remember. We still haven't decided what to do with the land just yet a lot of red tape with the area being the home to protected wildlife."

Armand nodded although he wasn't fully satisfied and knew when his dad was feeding him bullshit.

"Well, one more thing." Armand began placing his elbows on the table.

"No, business talk at the table," Hera whined pouting.

"Just one more sister and we can get back to your talks of fluttering about Tokyo."

Hera hissed discreetly giving him the middle finger; the gesture wasn't missed by their mother.

"Enough," Hemesh snapped, "go on dear," she directed her attention back to Armand as she visible swallowed a lump in her throat.

"I received something strange yesterday there's this name that I mentioned earlier, Madame Nikki and a check for a hundred thousand dollars along with a vial."

Armand watched the color drain from his father's face and beads of sweat populate the man's cupid's bow. He waited expectedly for an answer oblivious to the devious smirk Caesar hid in contents of his wine glass.

"The sender?" Maximillian shifted his gaze to his wife. She sat stoned face her eyes boring into his. He could sense her silent panic as his was rising as well.

"Didn't have a sender and no return address."

"Don't worry son, I'll have John look into it, could be a threat from another coven." His words were for Armand, but Maximillian's gaze was firmly locked onto Hemesh's.

Armand nodded stealing a glance at his mother who's beautiful sienna skin had taken on a sickly light grey hue.

"Interesting brother maybe I can take a look," Caesar chimed in, "do you have them here with you?"

"Leave it!" Maximillian shouted banging his open palm on the table rattling the dishes.

Hera jumped dropping her fork in the process.

Maximillian took his daughter's hand giving it a squeeze as he addressed Armand.

"I'm sorry, I'll take care of it."

"It's okay Daddy," Hera stated using the tone of voice that caused the hairs on the back of Armand's neck to rise.

He released her hand.

"Please, dinner, everyone eat. Your mother has gone through extraordinary pains to ensure everyone had something they enjoyed on the menu."

He smiled; it was pained as he swallowed hard. Armand picked up his fork turning his attention to the meal in front of him. His father only behaved that way when something bothered him. Usually, it was out of the old man's control that caused the cool and collected alpha to turn volatile.

Armand would let it go for now but would investigate further.

Dinner ended with promises to do this again. Hera was giddy as she went to her room leaving her brothers and parents together.

"Armand, do you have a moment?"

He was in the process of putting on his blazer when his father called for him.

"Of course."

"Good, my study."

Caesar lingered waiting and watched as Armand followed their father. He was hoping that he would be invited but when his father simply bade him good night his heart sank. His mother noticed his dejected mood and pulled him into a tight hug.

"He loves you too, Caesar." Hemesh mumbled into her youngest son's neck.

"He has a funny way of showing it."

Her youngest son pulled back looking down at the woman that had always made him feel just as loved and important despite being the second born male.

"You should stay longer. I can pull Hera out of her room, and we can play cards."

He chuckled, "no maybe next time, I need to get back to Evelyn."

His phone chimed it was his fiancé letting him know she was downstairs waiting.

Hemesh watched the retreating back of her son she felt the pain of existing in the shadows. Samira came to mind, and she quickly dismissed the thought of her sister. Even after all those years the woman haunted her.

Hera was ever a constant reminder of her older sister. Her daughter was like Samira not only in looks but in spirit as well. Hemesh considered it karma and had poured all the love she had for Samira onto her daughter hoping to make up for taking her life.

CAESAR LEFT HASTENING his steps when he exited the elevator. The car was out front, and he quickly climbed into the passenger seat. He barely closed the door before Evelyn sped off.

"How was dinner?"

He scoffed, "Armand mentioned the items he received and of course my father dismissed him, but I know my brother. Father's outburst will only push him to dig further."

He studied her as she sped through a stop sign.

"What's the matter?"

"We might have a problem. I spoke with Uri, the Russian Coven won't make a move with Maximillian's blessing and," she sighed gripping the wheel tighter, "my brother says the Chads want to back out. Everyone wants to talk to your father."

She took a sharp left as Caesar stared in horror. They needed more time. Things were progressing, but nowhere near the speed required.

He turned in his seat fighting against the seatbelt as Evelyn took another sharp turn this time on the ramp to the freeway.

"Fuck! We need more time! Tell your brother to stall." He bang his hand against the dashboard.

"I have. He's doing his best, but my father poses a problem as well, so does the table. Everyone want's your father's blessing on this."

Evelyn quickly changed lanes nearly clipping a silver Honda in the process. In one swift motion she was back in the right lane and took the exit overtaking a Prius causing the driver to hunk her horn in rage.

She whipped the McClaren into the underground parking garage. Once parked and the engine off she fell against the leather her gaze straight ahead.

"We need to move faster."

Caesar did the same and sighed. "I know."

ARMAND ENTERED HIS father's study and looked around. It had been so long since he had been here. The last time was telling his parents he was headed to Spain that was shortly after he graduated and two years after the incident.

He closed his eyes squinting hard. The name escaped him, but her face didn't. Even after seven years he couldn't forget the vacant stare into the abyss her sea green orbs glazed over. Internally he shook himself. *Enough.* His mother's voice echoed from earlier.

It was enough.

Maximillian watched him. He had practiced this speech over in this very room. Even having his valet stand in but now when presented with the man whom he was about to pass the mantle, his secrets unto he couldn't find those carefully crafted words.

"Sit."

Armand did as instructed taking residence on the leather sofa.

"How's life treating you? Are you glad to be home?"

Armand accepted the glass of bourbon as his father took a seat next to him.

"Fine and I must admit Father that no. I wasn't happy to be back but now, I'm glad I'm home for Mother, Caesar, Hera and," he paused the two men had never been affectionate, but Armand continued, "you."

Maximillian nodded.

"I'm glad you're home too son. Your mother missed you very much," he looked into his glass, "and so did I."

Armand chuckled, "I didn't think you wanted to see my face especially after all that happened." His voice dropped to a whisper, and he stared out the window at the night sky.

"No, son. Never. I was angry at the situation but not you."

"It felt like it; I thought I lost you and Mother's love. I thought the world had ended." Armand leaned back an attempt to hide his watery eyes. He had too much pride to openly cry.

His father sighed; his words had been harsh. He tried to be the opposite of his own father but instead replicated the toxic habits and ultimately chased away his eldest putting a strain on the relationship with his wife and that of his other children.

He was determined to right those wrongs.

"Armand, you and I haven't talked. I mean really talked. You'll be alpha someday." Maximillian stated his thumb lightly stroking the decorative bottom of the glass as he played with the pointed edge of the square base. His fingertips were numb the nerves deteriorating along with the rest of his body as the poison ravaged him.

"Yeah, but you know someday. I'm in no rush. You still got it old man." Armand raised his hand over his father's shoulder hesitating before giving it a firm squeeze. He pulled his hand back letting it fall into his lap.

"Well, who knows you may take the mantle sooner than you think."

Before Armand could probe further Maximillian stood, deciding to move on the cheery subjects.

"The Anaheim girl, Amelia."

Armand sat up shifting his weight, "what about her?"

"It's time to state your intentions."

He rolled his eyes, "the whole mate thing."

"Yes, son the mate thing, it's very important. One would say crucial." Maximillian's denim blue gaze bore into sand colored eyes.

He was serious once again.

"Do you have intentions with this young woman? Her father is a founding member and an old family friend." Despite the tension between himself and Charles he still considered the man a true friend.

"Wow, father, we went out on a date. I mean, I'll admit she's different than any woman I've known. I," he trailed off, "I don't know I've never been so unsure of myself. I could see myself with her." Armand admitted clutching the glass tighter.

Maximillian smirked, "I understand. It can be hard admitting your feelings being vulnerable. But being in love is a great and scary feeling."

"It that how you felt with Mom?"

He nodded moving toward the window his mind briefly going to Samira. His eyes snapped shut not now. The memory of her bloody body wrapped in the sheet would undue him in front of his son. Not tonight Hemesh didn't deserve to share their marital bed with a ghost.

"Yes," he whispered that familiar shame was back.

He loved his wife some days he found himself madly in love with her, but it was who she reminded him of, who she brought to mind when she was atop him in the early mornings her small hands on his chest as she rode him.

"It's your turn Armand. I want you to love someone. Do you love this girl?" He turned to face the man a confused expression was on his face as he stared at his father.

"It's too soon to tell but I think so, Father what's this about?" Armand stood.

"Nothing. We'll talk more. It's getting late." He gestured toward the grandfather clock, "we'll discuss more later."

Armand only nodded placing his glass on the bar cart as he passed. Everything felt off and he didn't know how to place his father's out of character behavior.

"Armand?"

"Yes?"

"If any more of those items arrive, you will let me know?"

Maximillian's eyebrows were raised leaving no room for questions.

Armand had many but knew not to press further.

"Of course, goodnight."

Armand sat in the back of the SUV there was more his father wasn't letting on. He would put Tina on it first thing Monday morning.

MAXIMILLIAN ENTERED his bedroom to find Hemesh still awake a book in her hand.

"I thought you would have been asleep."

She laughed, "you know me better than that. Besides it's still early."

She stood approaching him he enveloped her in his arms placing a kiss on her forehead.

"You want to talk about it now or later?"

"Now, or I won't sleep."

He released her and began removing his clothes. Hemesh watched from the corner of the bed her legs folded.

"I thought it was over finished."

"I know, I did too."

"Is Armand in danger?" Hemesh was starting to become upset at the thought her son may be in harm's way.

"I'm not sure but I won't let it get that far."

"Do you think it's Charles?"

"No, he has just as much to lose as I do. Maybe more."

"Who else knows?"

"I don't know," he removed his shirt.

She scoffed, "Well what do you know? Someone is digging up the past and putting my son in the middle of you and Charles' mess!" She raised her voice her expression hard.

"He's my son too Hem!"

Maximillian through up his hands, "he's my son too. I love him and I love you and don't want any of you to suffer because of what I did."

He stopped speaking abruptly to look down at his hands his fingers were twitching. Hemesh rushed to him the rage she had forgotten.

The petite Indian woman took his hands into her own holding them.

"I'm sorry for shouting. I'm scared that everything will come and the kids. What will happen to them?"

"There is no need for you to be afraid I will handle it. I always have." His tone was firm and Hemesh knew she would believe anything he told her.

He placed his forehead against hers. For a moment they enjoyed the silence as they fixated on their heartbeats.

"Did you tell him?" she whispered.

"No. I couldn't. Not now."

Hemesh sighed, "you must. You have tell all of them."

"Soon my love. Soon."

MONDAY MORNING CREPT in slowly and Caesar rose earlier than usual. He had put extended the invitation and waited. It didn't take long before his phone rang with a voice he hadn't heard since he was fifteen.

"I got your invitation."

No formal introductions the man meant business and Caesar liked that about Cain always had.

In a strange way young Caesar knew they were kindred spirits.

"There's a warehouse."

Cain quickly cut him, "No. I'm not meeting you at your little warehouse on Southside. I could walk into an ambush. No, I'll send you an address, oh and leave the African princess at home."

The call ended before he could ask when. After a few seconds a text came through with an address followed by NOW in bold letters. It was one he immediately recognized as the office building he owned. They rented out space to influencers and solo entrepreneurs that needed a desk, privacy, and an internet connection.

He arrived thirty minutes after he received the text. He figured he was being watched and had confirmation when his phone chimed with a text that simply read *310.*

He chuckled turning off the ignition and exiting the Porsche. The short walk to the sliding glass doors was a long one despite being less than twenty feet. The elevator ride seemed to somehow draw itself out seeming to stop at the floor in-between to let on a disinterested Instagram influencer muttering about declining followers under her breath.

The third floor and Caesar let out a breath he didn't realize he had been holding.

Beyond the glass he saw Cain. He had grown nearly two feet since Caesar last saw him. The round chubbiness from his younger days were gone replaced by a bulky frame that was the result of intense training.

"Caesar, not the DuBois I've wanted to see but you'll do I suppose, for now."

He gestured to the large glass enclosed office and Caesar stepped in not comfortable with having his back to a man with a score to settle.

"Well, I reached out to propose an allegiance. I understand you have a score to settle with my brother." He sat in the first chair to his left eager to get his eyes on the man.

"Really? What makes you think I am interested in anything other than settling that score as you say?" Cain paused staring intently at Caesar.

"I think you will be after you hear my proposal."

He chuckled, "if you think you can buy me off you're dumber than I thought. I'll be honest. You always came across as the kind of kid that didn't beat around the bush. My beef is with Armand and Maximillian. I loathe them both and I plan to reclaim what's mine." He hissed after speaking their names and Caesar figured this would be too easy.

"As do I."

Cain leaned back in his chair, "do tell."

"Armand is unfit to become alpha and my father is too tied to the old ways to bring about any real change. I have a vision. My father has always overlooked me for Armand. I am an outcast among them even Hera has more favor than I do as she is the only girl." He looked down attempting to rein in his emotions. He hadn't come consorting with the enemy to have a therapy session but find middle ground so that Cain could be used to expedite an agenda with an approaching deadline.

Cain laughed shaking his head.

"That's it? You're jealous and have Daddy issues."

"It's more than that. You want revenge for Danielle."

The smile dropped like a weight his features becoming hard once again.

"Yes, I know. I was around during the fallout, and I heard and saw many things. You also want to avenge your uncle Samuel. That scar, did Armand gave that to you? Was that his parting gift before he went off to Oxford to live carefree while everyone else dealt with the aftermath? You'll notice Cain like you I have done my homework."

Cain's jaw was clenched.

Caesar smirked, "now that I have your attention. We can discuss business. I know how my father became alpha, it's disgraceful especially coming from a man that preaches honesty and integrity but has put many wolves down for less offensive deeds. He's a hypocrite, and I'm not here to only offer a partnership but to provide assistance. Information that would take you days or weeks to get I could tell you now. As I know that my father didn't act alone."

Cain thought for a moment, the offer was enticing and would get him to the endgame a lot sooner. Camille had yet to provide anything tangible and he wrote the young woman off. She was a waste of time.

"What do you get out of this? You know I will kill them both."

It was Caesar's turn to chuckle, "I know. But as for my father death will come for him sooner than you think." He reached into his inner blazer pocket and produced a folded piece of paper. He handed it to Cain.

The man opened it reading intently before looking at Caesar.

"Turns out the poison that Samuel was injected with was transferred in a bite during the challenge into my father. Of course, it wasn't the same dose nor strength but just as deadly a kind of a final fuck you, you know." He wiggled his eyebrows as he sat back in his seat.

Cain sighed his gaze still on Caesar, "but still what do you get out of this? I plan to come for what was supposed to have been mine as the Wiltshire clan's only living male heir."

He held up his hand, "and you will have it. I plan to step aside recognize your authority and all that was taken from you."

"What's the plan?"

"We start with Armand he will be easy to deal with and I think you'll get a kick out of watching him suffer. As will I but we both know he will prove difficult to get next to as he has no known weaknesses. Until now."

Caesar watched as the scarred man sat up straighter his hand unfurling and curling into a tight fist.

"Go on."

"It appears my brother has claimed the Ms. Amelia Anaheim as his mate."

"I remember her from the party. We've met a time or two pretty little thing. A pretty, delicate little thing, so easily broken," he whispered.

"We use her to get him where we want him. Then you are free to enact your revenge on my father and his accomplice."

"The accomplice?"

Caesar nodded at this uneasy truce he had enacted, "Charles Anaheim."

Cain leaned back in the chair a gleam resided in his eyes that even unnerved Caesar.

Emotions

Armand sat holding the vial between his thumb and index fingers the check resting on his laptop keyboard forgotten for the moment. He pressed the call button and Tina entered a few seconds later holding a notebook.

Armand leaned forward, "Tina, have a seat please."

The young woman sat her pen at the ready.

"What I need is off the books," Armand began, "you did reconnaissance missions during your military time?"

Slowly she closed the neon pink Moleskin notebook and placed it along with the pen in her lap.

"Yes, I did."

"I may require you to do something outside of your normal duties as an assistant but that will rely heavily on your former training, are you comfortable with such a request? If not, tell me now and I won't ask again."

Tina thought for a moment before nodding.

"Good, come by the apartment this evening mention this to no one, seven o'clock."

"Yes sir. Is there anything else sir?" Tina asked standing near the door.

Armand didn't respond immediately watching a tall young man through the glass wall of his office. The blond wasn't a new face but new enough and due to Armand being so disgruntled when he returned from Spain, hadn't really noticed the latest edition until now.

"Tina don't look but there is a man standing next to Pauline's desk. Blonde, six two who is he?"

"Norman. He came exactly a week after you and I got here."

"Does he report to me?" Armand asked.

"No, he reports to your brother."

"Hmm, what does he do?"

"From outward appearances fetch coffee and chat up the interns but…" she trailed off her eyes now on the floor as she wrestled with her suspicions.

"Yes?"

"I wasn't sure sir, but he seems to be watching you."

"Why do you say?"

"Just something in my gut tells me he's not to be trusted and I've seen him lurking once or twice where he shouldn't be."

Armand thought for a moment, "could be a plant by my brother. Keep your eyes and ears open, that's all."

"Yes sir."

Tina spun on her heels leaving Armand with more questions and confusion. He continued to watch the young man as he took a box of coffee pods in the kitchenette before he returned taking a seat at the empty desk that faced his office.

"What are you up to Caesar?"

IT HAD BEEN OVER A week since the conversation with his father. His feelings weren't letting up and even if they had he would have found his way back to her. His father had been right. It was time, and no other compared. He wasn't sure if they were fated, but he had chosen his mate and tonight he would make it know before the pack.

Armand squared his shoulders he was quickly losing his nerve.

The heir had Tina stand in as he practiced the proposal in his apartment but now given tonight was the equivalent of his debut performance at Carnegie Hall, he was becoming nervous.

Armand sighed this wasn't his apartment and Tina was two states away tracking down the information he requested.

He fingered the velvet box in his left pocket the diamond had been ethically sourced from a jeweler he met while in Spain. His gaze lingered on her. Amelia's skin glowed under the lights as she moved through the crowd mingling effortlessly, even former rivals loosened up and Amelia had the young women laughing and chatting.

Yes, she was the one. There was no doubt on his part.

He took a fluke of champagne from a passing waiter and waited nearly a minute before clearing his throat.

Silence trickled over the room in a wave as everyone turned their attention on him.

"As everyone knows it comes a time in every man's life where he finds a partner. As for me it has taken…a while."

Everyone laughed his mother stood with her hands to her chest in anticipation. Hemesh's eyes had grown dark and watery, the Coven matriarch had waited a long time for this moment. Her eldest seemed happy and for a moment the carefree little boy that was afraid of the dark was standing before the crowd. Public speaking was another fear he managed to hide quite well before he was able to conquer it.

Max gripped the glass he held tighter he had hoped things with Charles' eldest would have fizzled out and hadn't known that his son had claimed the girl as his mate. Although ignorant of his son's intentions he wasn't surprised; when his son was set on something he pursued it relentlessly, Amelia had been no different.

He brought his gaze to rest on Amelia's parents. Diane could have been knocked over with a feather his friend looked apprehensive. Maximillian understood why. He shared in his friend's guilt. His gaze shifted yet again to rest on his son once he heard him call Amelia's name. The woman approached slowly her eyes locked on Armand. It was easy to tell she was just as taken with his son as he was with her.

Diane was smiling as she turned to look at her husband. The guilt Charles felt was still strong. He felt as if he request all those years ago had been unfair, but he was grateful he didn't have to push Max further than necessary. He would have hated to make an enemy of his oldest friend.

Armand took Amelia's hand, Caesar recognizing the moment stepped forward and took the glass from his brother before quickly stepping back. He eyed Evelyn this impromptu proposal solidified the value the young woman had in the continuation of their plan. Finally, they had a weakness to exploit.

Evelyn smiled as if she had read his thoughts before her gaze shifted to the couple.

Armand took a knee and a collective gasp fell over the attendees. Several members exchanged whispers before they were harshly shushed.

"Amelia Delilah Anaheim, will you consent to be my bride?" he asked holding her gaze.

Hemesh's cheeks were damp, and she had never seen her son so unsure of himself. She moved forward in anticipation of the answer. Diane had let out an audible gasp before clamping her hand over her mouth.

"Yes," Amelia breath out heavily and Armand took in a deep breath needing air. He wasn't sure if he would have been able to carry on if she had stated otherwise.

Hemesh began clapping as she approached the couple. The others followed suit beginning to gather around the pair. A small path was made as Diane, Charles and Maximilian made their way through the crowd.

Armand pulled Amelia into a deep kiss causing the young ladies to ooh and ahh.

Diane stood silently; she couldn't find words to express how happy she was in the moment. When the pair broke their kiss, she grabbed Armand and pulled him into a tight embrace.

"Congratulations!" she pushed him at arm's length before pulling him back in for a hug.

"Mom, please," Amelia spoke partially out of embarrassment and jealousy. She didn't anyone touching him.

Diane released him and turned to her daughter. She grabbed her and repeated the cycle of pulling her in a tight embrace. Amelia tried to wiggle free but was caged in when her two brothers joined their mother wrapping their arms around both women.

Hemesh even joined in pulling her son in for a brief hug. Caesar and Evelyn stayed on the peripheral opting to delve out verbal praises to the recently engaged.

They stood nearly a minute before Armand stepped forward tapping Mason on the shoulder.

Mason backed away from the embrace his hands in the air mock surrender, "sorry bro. Step back Lam, Armand wants his bride."

Liam hopped back laughing wiggling his eyebrows suggestively. Diane released Amelia holding her at arm's length giving her a once over.

"Don't tease them," she clasped her hands together.

Charles and Maximillian locked eyes staring at one another during the exchange of pleasantries. Hemesh approached her husband placing her hand on his shoulder. She gave it a light squeeze before rising on her tiptoes and whispering in his ear, "not here."

Reluctantly he broke eye contact and turned to his son. Armand waited watching his father carefully. Amelia stood nervously to his side and reached for her mother's hand out of habit.

The two eyed each other and Maximillian out of character grabbed his son and pulled him into a hug. His father hadn't shown him such emotion since he was seven years old.

Hemesh watched her hands over her mouth as more tears flowed down her cheeks. Armand would never admit it, but this gesture meant more to him than he would let on.

Slowly they disengaged and Maximillian motioned for the waiters. As if engaged in a sequenced dance the tuxedo clad servers approached presenting trays of champagne.

Maximillian took one.

"I would like to give my gift early, rarely do I overlook tradition but tonight I will make an exception," he turned to Armand, "as my eldest and my heir. Your mother had planned a very nice and very expensive event for this in the coming weeks. But I figure why wait, you are ready. I am stepping aside and naming you Alpha."

Maximillian waved his hand nonchalantly, "we can finish all the necessary paperwork and the details of rites and ceremony later."

Many gasped, several council members exchanged glances unhappy with the impromptu announcement and unauthorized engagement that had taken place. They would address their alpha at a later time.

Armand stood stoic his eyes had grown watery, and he had to look down briefly to collect himself. The hall erupted in applause and Armand once again closed the gap between them and embraced his father.

Caesar and Evelyn joined in the applause but exchanged worried glances, their timeline would have to be accelerated considerably, they would need Armand removed before he was officially recognized by the council.

The celebration lasted for nearly four hours and would have lasted longer but the expensive liquor and food ran out therefore it was time to close shop for the evening.

Evelyn and Caesar were the first to leave citing business meetings and early calls to make the following morning.

The two strode hand in hand until they reached the black SUV. The driver quickly opened the door as the couple slid onto the leather seat.

"I thought he wasn't going to propose until next week?" Evelyn snatched her hand out of his and angled her body to face him.

Caesar held up his hand, "I didn't know. Armand is unpredictable." He sighed.

"You're his brother you're supposed to know him better than anybody. We have too much on the line for everything to fall through. My brother has convinced the Chadian Coven and the Nigerians to wait but not for long. My sister right now is in Spain meeting with delegates about this international wolf union you've dreamt up."

"That you co-signed by the way Evie. I am not some crazy man with delusions of grandeur," he sat up in the seat reaching for her hand, "I have a vision, we have a vision. You as well as I know that over the decades we have had to hide in the shadows, only mingle amongst ourselves. With this plan we can start to accumulate some real power. Money will only get us so far with the humans."

The corners of Evelyn's full lips turned upward slightly. She didn't love Caesar, that much of their arranged engagement had been mutual but they had a deep respect for one another. Unlike her previous betrothal, Caesar listened to her ideas and respected her opinions. He made it clear he was looking for more than a child bearer and beautiful woman on his arm; she was an equal. With him, she didn't have to hide her intelligence.

"You're right. I just don't like curve balls."

"I know sweetheart."

"Where are we with Camille?"

"For now, I think we should put her on ice. Focus on Cain."

"Why? I thought the plan was to use her until we got to the point we needed."

"Camille may have a change of heart and besides he's the one with a bone to pick with my father and Armand."

"You've followed her again?"

"No, her sister or rather half-sister has been looking into some things on Camille's behalf. The half breed has been looking through archives and asking the wrong questions to the right people. She could expose everything."

"You think she knows?"

"No, but if the sister keeps at it she will. If anyone finds out we are organizing an international union of werewolves behind the Council's back without the knowledge of my father, I'd be exiled. It would be a miracle if I'm not killed."

He sighed rolling his eyes. "I hate that everything is still stuck in the old ways. We can move forward into a new day."

Evelyn thought for a moment staring out the window beyond her fiancé, "let me deal with Camille. If she doesn't cooperate, I will find permanent means to keep her quiet. As for the half-sister, I may have something. You say she's a half breed, correct?"

"Yes." He raised his eyebrow curious.

"Half breeds aren't allowed in the coven, right?"

His smile was devilish as he followed where she was leading.

"No, they're not."

She leaned backward into the leather, "we could offer her Camille's counsel seat. This half-sister of hers wants what any child wants – acceptance."

She stared at him giving him time to object.

He sat quietly for a few seconds before he spoke, "good, we can contain the sister. Let's put her in our back pocket. As for Camille, she's just about served her purpose anyway and that might be what we need. It will send a message to Armand. But try to reason with her first if not, we will dispense with her sooner than planned."

He smiled leaning in placing a kiss on her lips. Evelyn chuckled pulling him closer deepening the kiss and the two began pulling at the designer fabric covering each other's bodies. They only stopped enough to get out of the back of the SUV but continued in the elevator as the footman stood in the corner ignoring them.

They finished on the floor of the large bedroom. It wasn't a love making session but simply to satisfy their primal needs strengthening their bond and pursuit of power. Children had not been discussed.

There was no need neither had the desire despite much meddling from both sides.

Second Thoughts

Camille had thought on everything she and Gianna discussed over the last three days. Normally, she had the nerve and will but now with the walls closing in she didn't want to help Caesar nor Cain.

She rolled over grabbing her phone from the nightstand. She would make the call and she would do it now.

He answered on the first ring, Camille had expected nothing less she figured a man as ruthless as he would sleep with it next to his ear.

"Yes?" the tone was clipped and bored.

"I need to speak with you."

"Camille," Caesar spoke the name turning to look at Evelyn as she brought her gaze from the passing cityscape to Caesar.

"What can I do for you?"

"The deal is off."

"I don't understand."

"You heard me, I will remain silent. I assure you I won't interfere with your plans nor go anywhere near Armand, but I won't help you either."

"Why the change of heart Camille? When you, Evelyn and I sat down at dinner we agreed to usher in change. I want you to be a part of something great."

"Look, if you succeed, I will be of service in any way I can, but I won't help with this. It's..." she trailed off.

"Wrong?" he filled in the silence, "I understand. Well, Camille what about your partner Cain? Does he know?"

She sighed, "Not yet, I have pretty much ghosted him."

"Well, you should tell him. Be firm like you were with me. He will appreciate you being forthright."

"You're taking this better than expected."

"Camille I am a businessman you know how many deals fall through. You're in real estate I'm sure you can relate besides I don't punish people for being adults."

She paused entirely believing him, "thank you and good night."

"Goodnight." He ended the call and faced Evelyn.

"She's out."

"In more ways than one." Evelyn stated, "what now? She knows entirely too much to just have her out and about. It makes me nervous."

Caesar began to dial, "don't worry my love, it's already taken care of."

"Cain, we have a problem. Camille, she's out. I'm sure you know what needs to be done." The call ended and he sighed.

He laid the phone in his lap and placed his hands over his face, "my God between my father, Armand and this bitch I'm about at my wits end!"

He shouted causing the driver to look up in the rearview mirror before shifting his gaze back to the road.

"I know." She placed her hand on his thigh, "it's kind of, I don't know, sweet. He wants to protect us."

"No, my father wants us two floors down for control."

"He didn't sound like a man that wanted control. The old man really cares about you."

"No, he cares about his heir, Armand," he dropped his hands, "do you know why he pulled me to the side?"

"No, but I have a feeling you're going to tell me."

"He asked why the wedding is so far out and why you aren't at least pregnant by now."

Evelyn busted out laughing gripping her stomach as she leaned forward, "really? Wow!"

"No it's not funny; it was embarrassing. He said people are going to start thinking something was wrong with me that I couldn't even get my fiancée pregnant."

The laughing spell was over, and she simply stared at him a small smirk on her face.

"Well your father isn't the only one. My parents have been asking as well."

There was a long silence.

"We haven't discussed it. But when you're alpha they will be expected, required rather. We wouldn't want all of our hard work and planning to be in vain."

"No, I wouldn't," he whispered, "but what if you know we have two sons and they're like us. Me and Armand?" He stopped leaving the question in the air hoping he wouldn't have to explain.

Evelyn regarded him he had never looked so unsure and small.

She took his hands, "they won't be. We will be there and do the right thing by them both."

He nodded and placed a kiss on her lips. Her lips parted tongue darting out to meet his. Her hand found its way into his trousers as his hand snaked around her back unzipping her dress.

The driver ignored them his eyes never leaving the road as he heard sounds of pleasure from the back row.

"I THOUGHT I SHOULD tell you in person, I am no longer helping you with this, Armand thing." She stared at Cain waiting.

He chuckled, "now all those weeks ago you went through so much time and trouble to seek me out so I could join you in taking down the man that has been using you only for your delectable little body. I thought we wanted to expose that family for the frauds and murderers they are, now you want to back out, why?"

Camille sighed and looked around, it was nearly midnight and although she had brought the pearl handle Glock as extra protection it was under the driver's seat and useless to her.

She thought the parking deck was a good place but now she was regretting the decision. The space was too enclosed and there weren't many places to maneuver. Her hair bristled and she could sense he was on the verge of a shift.

"I don't want to be involved with whatever you and Cesar have going on. This is about dynasty and legacy things that have nothing to do with me."

He laughed the sound danced over the empty spaces before it bounced off the concrete walls.

"I understand."

The simple statement caught her off guard.

She licked her lips out of habit, "really? What's the catch?"

"No catch Camille," he shrugged his shoulders, "I understand. It's scary."

She uncrossed her arms.

"Ok, we wash our hands of each other. I won't tell Armand or any of the DuBois.'"

"Of course."

She turned wanting to get behind the wheel and out of the garage.

"Camille."

She whipped around her eyes growing large at the handgun that was pointed at her. Cain fired three shots in rapid succession before the tall blonde had time to react. She fell against the G Wagon gasping for air. The bullets hit the intended target lodging themselves in the center of her chest.

Cain slowly closed in the few feet of separation and stood over her.

He slowly lowered himself to his knees and leaned forward bringing his mouth near her ear, "you can't walk away from something like this, you're just like Danielle."

Camille gargled struggling to speak, "it was you." She stated with much difficulty gasping between words as spittle of blood coated her chin and tip of her nose.

He shifted his eyes locked with the fading green irises of hers, "yeah, I guess it was. Just like you she chose Armand. But she was mine I couldn't let go so easily and let a DuBois win again."

"You framed him," she choked out nearly strangling on blood.

"Well, that part was pretty easy to do. Armand has always been an arrogant ass, too busy to notice what's going on around him. You know what I learned, we wolves are hardy but slip us three horse tranquilizers and we go down like a sack of potatoes."

He was grinning finding his joke amusing.

He stood, "only thing I regret Camille is not getting rid of Armand when I had the chance. I should have ripped out his throat instead."

Cain ran his eyes over Camille's body sucking his teeth, "such a waste," before he raised the gun and fired two more shots into her chest and a third into her forehead.

He left her body in the parking garage the early morning shift workers would no doubt have found her by now.

During the drive to his office he hissed, Caesar's timeline was too slow and besides he was never one to work with another. He wanted Armand and he wanted him now. He stole a quick glance at his phone his mind shifting like he was in and out of traffic.

"Amelia, Amelia," he repeated her name like a song chorus as he gripped the phone tighter. Anger was descending on him like a fine mist, and he steered off into the underground parking garage.

IT WAS AROUND NOON when she received the call, Cain wanted to meet for dinner to discuss his contribution to her organization. With her mind preoccupied with Armand and the nights they shared following the proposal, she had accepted the invitation without much thought.

Armand was pulled from his computer by a rapping at the door to his office. It was Caesar and he smiled.

"Good morning Brother, what do I owe the pleasure?

"May I?" Caesar's tone was serious, and he entered shutting the door behind him. He stood at the desk looking down at his brother hands behind his back.

"I take it from your demeanor you haven't heard the news."

Armand's expression fell and he stood, "what is it?"

Caesar sighed trying to ensure he looked as convincing as possible.

"Camille was found dead this morning in a parking garage."

Armand slowly sank to his chair his features hard. Although he had never loved the woman it didn't do anything to dull the small ache in his chest. It was guilt at how things ended between them. He was arrogant and wrong now his chance to make amends was forever lost.

"How?"

"She was shot multiple times, possible robbery."

Caesar watched his brother a small smirk forming.

"I'll reach out to the family. I'll leave you to your thoughts."

Once alone he stood rushing into the private bathroom where he sat on the toilet. For the first time in years, the man that wore an aloof and tough exterior like one of the expensive tailored suits sobbed into his hands.

IT WAS JUST BEFORE dawn when Gianna got the call. Oddly enough it was her mother. She figured the call was going to be a warning to stay away from Camille, so she was hesitant to answer.

"Yes?" Gianna whispered. She wasn't sure why she was nervous after all these years and only after one introduction.

There was sobbing on the other end before a woman cleared her throat.

"Gianna?"

"Yes, this is she."

"Camille is dead."

Gianna gasped nearly dropping the phone.

"What happened? She,"

A loud strained cry echoed in her ear, "it's your fault!" Elizabeth hissed on the other end. "I knew you were trouble when I had you. I...," more cries and Elizabeth was struggling to speak.

"I told her to stay away from you."

"Elizabeth, I don't'"

"Don't say my name!"

Gianna fought back tears as she placed her hand over her mouth to keep from screaming.

"I hate that you feel that way but Camille got mixed up in something that was beyond you and me. It was dangerous and I tried to get her to stop. I..." she trailed off unsure how to proceed or is she should.

Elizabeth had gone silent, "why didn't you try harder?" She whispered her voice had taken on a resigned tone and Gianna closed her eyes shaking her head.

She wasn't sure why she didn't push harder sooner. The damage was done and by the time Camille no longer wanted to play this dangerous game she knew too much no body worth their weight in salt would let her live.

"I don't know. She stopped maybe they found out and...did this. How?"

"She was shot, Gianna. Executed! My baby," she sobbed.

Silence filled the space between them, and Gianna had to steal a glance at her phone to ensure her mother hadn't hung up.

"I don't want to ever see you again."

The tears finally fell. The statement was too familiar the exact one the very woman on the other end had said to her a little over twenty years ago.

"The funeral, can I at least come? She was my sister; I have the right to say goodbye."

"Fine, but after that I want you gone. Out of our lives you have brought nothing but destruction."

Before she could respond the call was ended and Gianna threw the phone on the table and began to sob her shoulders moving up and down sporadically.

Gianna cried for nearly an hour before her resolve once again harden. They were rich entitled, they got rid of things that were an inconvenience. Her birth had been one of those and her mother discarded her. Now, she wasn't sure if she would attend Camille's funeral.

The doorbell rang she wasn't in the mood to receive guests and it crossed her mind to not answer. The chime echoed throughout the house once again and she rose from the couch and stumbled toward the front door.

Ginna didn't bother with the peep hole because if she had it was a strong possibility she wouldn't have answered.

A well-dressed man stood his perfectly straight teeth showing and Gianna swore she thought they shone in the afternoon sunlight. Her mood took another dive. She recognized him as the youngest DuBois son, Caesar.

She scoffed, "you make house calls now for murder? Am I next on your hit list?"

He chuckled, "no. What happened to Camille was an unfortunate accident, a robbery gone horribly wrong; the news said so." That used car salesman smile was back, and Gianna wondered how this man ever made it as one of the top businessmen in the city.

"Bullshit," she hissed, "the news is about as reliable as a Cadillac with two wheels."

He laughed, "may I come in?"

"NO."

"Very well. You may want to invite me in after you hear what I have to propose. Your half wolf, correct?"

"Yeah, everyone keeps reminding me."

"A change is coming where your kind will be allowed to join and fellowship with others like them. You would have access to resources that you could use for your children and your PI business. They are several members that would pay handsomely for your discretion and skills."

He paused waiting for a reaction that never came, he continued hoping mention of the council seat would sweeten the pot.

"My plan is to integrate more half wolves with the Red Bloods. Great change would come, and I would like to offer you a seat on the council. You could be part of that change."

She laughed, "I won't be dragged into your web. Your father had someone killed that was close to me and that I loved very much he should pay for that."

"What my father has done in the past is unfortunate and although I am his son, I have a certain code of ethics. I am more than willing to make amends on his part. What can I offer to get you to join us? Don't you want elevation for your children?"

Gianna watched him, he was good and maybe had he caught her ten years ago she would have said yes without a second thought but now after all she had uncovered the whole lot of them was dangerous. The Coven only served as a safe haven for their kind's nefarious individuals. There was a reason less than half of the American werewolf population were members.

They couldn't be trusted.

"How many ways do I have to put my answer? No. I'm not interested not now; not anymore." Gianna moved to shut the door, but Cesar's reflexes were faster, and he had his hand out preventing her from closing it.

His features had shifted slightly, and Gianna could tell this wasn't a man that was used to hearing the word *no* often. She stood up straighter.

"I was waiting for the real Caesar to show up, is there where you kill me? Or are you going to call someone else to do it? Maybe Daddy? Or Cain?"

He dug his nails into the door, "I would be carefully Gianna. I would hate for a mother of four to come up missing; children that young need their mother. A word of advice stop asking questions you don't want the answers to. I would hate for you to end up next to Camille, remember you have a lot more to lose than she did."

He removed his hand from her door and ran it through his hair before he turned on his heel leaving Ginna standing in the threshold. She quickly shut the door. She was shaking, she did have a lot to lose and let out a long breath before pulling in another one.

GIANNA DIDN'T SLEEP much that night nor the two that followed. She went as far having the children stay home from school and they missed three soccer games. She didn't want to take any chances. Basically, the mother of four had resigned herself that she would never get the justice that her Aunt Nikki deserved. She couldn't avenge the woman she had considered a mother.

Like before there was a knock on her door. This time softer lighter. Gianna made sure to use the peep hole and was met with the image of a tall slender brown skinned woman.

She hesitantly opened the door the .38 in her hand resting against her thigh.

"Yes?"

"Gianna?" The woman asked, extending a card.

"Good morning my name is Tina Gates and I'm looking for information. If my sources are correct you have a lot of it I can use regarding the Coven."

Gianna stood momentarily dumbfounded this was a human asking about the organization. She eased her head out around the door looking around.

"Who sent you?"

"I know the basics; you are half wolf. Your mother is Elizabeth Knight, I know and my condolences for your sister Camille."

"How do you know? Are you a PI?"

"No, the man I work for wants the truth. He means you no harm. Armand DuBois."

Gianna sighed, "makes sense. Come in." She opened the door wider. She quickly placed the gun in the waistband of her leggings and covered it with her shirt. The host wasn't comfortable putting the gun away until she learned more regarding the aim of the lady's boss and the woman herself.

Gianna led the young woman to the worn couch and the two sat.

"Forgive me Miss Gates, but everything I have found out about that family is nothing good." She shifted her weight. She wasn't sure why she was nervous all of a sudden.

"Please Tina. In light of all of the things that have happened, Mr. DuBois simply wants answers."

"So, he sent you to get them?" She asked her eyebrows meeting her hairline.

"Yes. I'll be forth coming with you, and I expect the same."

Gianna nodded.

"What do you want to know?"

The two talked for hours Gianna giving Tina all of the information she had including recorded calls and even told her of the visit from the younger DuBois brother.

It would be an understatement to say that Tina's jaw dropped a few times throughout her talk with Gianna. This was huge and dangerous. The middle aged mother had been more than forth coming giving all she had which was like a forbidden treasure trove and Tina had jumped headfirst in reading everything handed to her.

Tina left wanting to get on a flight to Gianna's contact in New Hampshire. She would be visiting with the last of the Wiltshire Clan, save Cain Lewis.

ARMAND HAD GRIEVED for a little over a week as he waited for Tina to make it back. He had received the update that she had what he was looking for and more. He had taken a few days off work to not only grieve for Camille but prepare himself. Her murder had broken something free in him that brought with it years of pent-up emotion.

He had a nagging feeling the information would upend his world. Armand knew it would change everything. Amelia had stayed with him several days sensing the change in mood. She had stayed on the edges, and he had appreciated the silent support. He wasn't sure how to explain that his grief was related to the murder of a former lover.

After a week he ushered his soon to be bride home. Part of tradition Amelia would stay with her family no doubt partaking in the Anaheim Clan's own celebrations.

A soft knock followed by a key being inserted into the lock drew him out of thoughts and he quickly took in a deep breath, it was Tina and his body relaxed.

"In here," he yelled out.

"Armand, I have, woah!" She stopped short noticing that he was sitting on the bed nude.

She had observed many curious and eccentric habits of her wolf born boss. Tina was a little curious as to why this caught her off guard.

"Umm," she shook her head and continued, "I have everything in my bag."

His eyes had shifted and were glowing in the dim light. Armand patted the bed as he stood.

"Okay?" She placed her bag near where his ass had been only a few seconds prior and started pulling everything. The folders laying them on the bedspread. The papers seemed endless as Armand's heart began to beat faster as Tina continued pulling items from the black bag..

He watched his breathing becoming shallow as she pulled out a rolled up piece of parchment inside of a glass tube. He had never seen it but he had a sinking feeling he knew what it was. glass tube of aged parchment.

Tina turned presenting it to her boss as he stood watching intently.

"What's this?"

"The most important piece of the puzzle and the possible catalyst for all that has happened."

Armand slowly took it from her outstretched hand and held it against his chest.

"Thank you, Tina, take the rest of the month."

"Sir?"

"Take the month." He repeated the command leaving no room to argue.

"I don't want you caught in the cross hairs when the shit hits the fan, and if my brother is the one behind all of this I don't want you on his hit list."

She nodded placing the bag on her shoulder.

"By the door is an envelope you will find plane tickets and a debit card with account information. Disappear. Understand?"

She stood, the gravity of the situation weighing on her as she watched her boss. He usually hid it very well, but he was shaken she would say he was scared. It didn't happen often. Tina could only recount once during her seven-year tenure that she had seen the emotion displayed before.

"Yes sir. Thank you Armand and be careful."

His eyes were on all that was on the bed as he addressed her, "plane leaves at six."

She smiled nodding, "of course sir," was spoken as she left leaving him to sort through decades of murder and treason that was displayed against the pristine black silk.

He began with the document in his hand. It was the original decree, how the human managed to get her hands on such an item was beyond him, but he would have his accountant place more money into her account.

He read it not only once but four times, after each reading he would go over the decree that was available to them all and compare it to the original. Everything lined up and one would get bored with how each stroke match along with the verbiage between the two documents. Except the Doctrine of Challenge and Rite of Lineage.

They, it didn't align nor make any sense. No wolf worth his fur would have agreed to knowingly take away their lineage's inheritance and hand all that power over willingly.

Before the Coven, wolves had killed for less.

He pondered on the autopsy report, it was clear the former alpha had been poisoned. Samuel only ever saw one doctor in his adulthood and that was Charles Anaheim, the coroner that performed the repeat autopsy noted a needle mark that prior to death hadn't healed no doubt a side effect from the vile that was injected into his veins. Only person that had the opportunity was his doctor.

Amelia's father.

His father's actions over the years became clear. Cain had been right. He was an illegitimate heir. He had no claim to the mantle of alpha nor did his father. That piece bothered him but not as much as the murder of his Aunt Samira by Samuel.

If the accounts were correct, the man had been infatuated with his young bride to be and not one that would have murdered a woman. Tossed her aside yes but even taking a life unjustified was beneath the arrogant man.

Tina had been nothing short of thorough. Her notes rivaled those of any Rhodes scholar, and he studied long into the night. What pieces Tina had been unable to put together his brother and Camille's half-sister had. Not only was his father a murderer but so was his mother.

He needed more. *What was his brother up to?*

HE STAYED LATE AT WORK, going through the company's financials, and looking into his brother's dealings. Armand knew his brother was a low life, but he didn't know how far his brother would stoop.

Millions were reallocated to several unfamiliar accounts in Europe and Africa. A few of those millions ending up somewhere in Spain. Other amounts were shown on the books as donations to something called The League.

His phone chimed and barely able to tear his eyes away from the screen he glanced at the screen. It was from Amelia, and he quickly picked it up and opened the message.

He had hoped the woman had changed her mind on the time apart and he feared she would refuse leaving him worse off than he'd ever been before.

Armand leapt from his chair knocking it over. It was a photo of Amelia tied up and an address. Luckily he didn't need it as he nearly ran from the office taking the stairs nearly jumping down a flight at a time until he was on the bottom level. He raced to the car sliding behind the wheel and firing up the engine.

The phone rang it was Amelia's number and he quickly answered.

"Amelia!" he screamed.

He was greeted with a deep chuckle and reflexively the hairs on his body rose rubbing uncomfortably against the fabric of his shirt. He loosened his tie as his airway become narrower.

"Cain."

"Who else?"

More chuckling and Armand could hear Amelia in the background. Her voice sounded strained as if gaged and he suddenly became overcome with panic and fear.

"If you hurt her, I swear to the goddess," more laughter.

"But I intend to, Armand. Did you not get the gift I sent you? A life for a life, you took Danielle now I am going to take Amelia. But not after I have a little fun," he laughed and hung up before Armand could respond.

He threw the phone on the seat and reversed out of the reserved parking space. The eldest DuBois was unaware that he had been followed and a set of eyes was on him.

Norman pulled the cell from his breast pocket and hit the number for speed dial. Caesar picked up not bothering to give a greeting.

"He's on the move."

"Good." Caesar spoke as he held back a moan as the woman took him deeper in her mouth.

"You want me to follow."

"Yes," he hissed as Evelyn's teeth grazed his shaft, "um, but under no circumstance are you to interfere. You know what to do for your scent cover. Let Cain finish what he started all those years ago," he closed his eyes, "I have to go."

He ended the call and Norman pulled up the tracker he had placed on Armand's car and followed in the dark SUV.

"Wait, sweetheart wait."

Evelyn rested her elbows on his thighs as she stared up at him.

He placed the cell back to his ear.

"Cain, he's on the way. Finish it."

"I plan to; I'll call you to come and collect his body when it's over."

He hung up before Caesar could reply.

He was silent as he locked eyes with his fiancée.

"Should I feel bad?" he asked his expression was one of confusion as he shifted his gaze toward his computer.

"Do you?" she asked rubbing her hand down his chest.

He smirked looking back at her, "no. not at all."

She smiled as he pulled her up into his lap.

"Now, let's work on this baby our parents keep asking about."

The two chuckled as he lifted her up onto the desk.

Armand arrived in a record forty five minutes despite the traffic. It was the cabin and he quickly shed his clothes and allowed the change to take over. He approached from the rear of the old structure coming through what was once a bedroom.

He chuckled hearing the soft padding of his best friend. Cain inhaled deep, the scent of Armand's anger and trepidation mixed with the woman's fear caused him to lick his lips as he placed his hand on Amelia's shoulder.

He opened his eyes quickly wrangling in his arousal and the erection that had started to form due to the unease from the woman tied up next to him.

Armand was closer and Cain had his hands in her hair pulling at the root. She hissed in pain as tears stung her eyes. He leaned down sniffing her as Armand shift into human form and entered the room.

He was about to charge when Cain spoke.

"I wouldn't Armand." He stated looking at his former best friend as he placed his hand on the back of Amelia's neck.

"I could snap her little neck. He hissed in her ear.

"But where is the fun in that? No, I'm going to do you like your boyfriend did Danielle. But first I'm going to rip his legs off," he whispers harshly pointing at Armand.

"Then," he brought his mouth to Amelia's face licking her cheek. Amelia in vain tried to move back but he held on tighter causing her to cry out once again.

"Then I'm going to fuck you. Safe to say you're no virgin, not anymore. Armand made sure if that didn't, he sweetheart, like he always does," he glared at Armand his teeth bared in what one could interpret as a smile, "you're going to watch. Then I'm going to rip your throat out." He whispered the last statement in her ear spittle coating her ear lobe.

"Cain that's enough your problem is with me not her."

"You're right." He released his hold on Amelia her head snapping forward at the sudden release of tension.

Cain's tall husky frame approached Armand's.

"I think I'll just kill you and I'll keep the girl. Once I'm done ripping you apart I'm coming for Papa Max. I'll kill him before the poison will."

Armand's expression fell this was a first surely his father would have told him.

"You're lying!" Armand shouted causing the aged and weather-beaten windowpanes to rattle.

"Ah," Cain mocked placing a hand over his heart, "Prince Armand doesn't know why he was called back from Spain. You think anyone wanted you back?"

"Fuck you!" He hissed.

"You already did that. You and your family. Murderers all of you, ill-gotten gains. None of this is supposed to be yours. I'm the true heir! If your father hadn't poisoned my uncle you wouldn't be in line for alpha. You are an illegitimate heir."

Cain spread his arms wide as the men continued to stare down one another. Armand needed to time his attack at the wrong angle his nemesis could move causing him to charge into Amelia. He was sure given her siting position and the force of the attack her spine would snap. The man was too close, and she would get hurt in the process.

"I've never known you to be a liar Cain."

"Not lies dear brother but facts. Does Madame Nikki ring a bell? The vial, the check for a 100 grand?"

Armand paused thinking back to all the items he received. His mood shifted from anger to confusion in an eyes blink.

"It was you. I should have known coward as always lurking in the shadows."

"No, Armand. Not me someone closer." He laughed the sound bouncing off the bare walls.

"Think Armand, think. But that's never been your strength. Has it? A coward you say. I'm not the one that ran after Danielle's body was found."

Armand growled, "I didn't kill Danielle!"

"Well, it sure looked that way. You couldn't stand that she chose me over you. What, you couldn't handle that she wasn't impressed by your good looks? News flash not every woman wants to fuck you, Armand."

Armand chuckled, "no I don't think you could handle the fact she didn't want you. She came there of her own free will. I was already there alone when she knocked on the door. She wanted me to tell you to stay away. So much for your girlfriend."

"Lies! You lured her there and you know it!"

"No, she didn't want you. Who could blame her with you following her around campus. Paying to get her schedule. You were a sick fuck! A weirdo! You were one then and you are one now."

"Shut up!"

Armand could tell that he was getting to Cain he decided to press further aiming for the tender places only a best friend knew how.

His father's illness forgotten for now.

Cain growled and lunged for Armand. He pivoted causing Cain to miss. This allowed him enough time to change.

Amelia watched in fear and fascination as the two continued to fight. Somewhere in the scrimmage a paw was raised, and a splatter of blood landed across her face. The scent was unfamiliar, not the deep husky tones of Armand.

It was Cain's and she sat up straighter tuning her ears toward the room in which the pair had fallen into.

After several minutes a great howl of victory was heard, and she steeled herself for the chance that Armand was not the victor.

He emerged across the threshold and staggered. Half of his body was covered in blood a large scar extended from his left shoulder across his chest ending at his upper abdomen. He hissed with each movement using the last of his energy, he rushed toward her collapsing at her feet.

Amelia felt the chains around her ankles give way and soon Armand was using her bare thighs as support as he laid his upper body in her lap and reached behind her.

She caught the glimmer of a key and sighed in relief. Once her hands were free she pushed at his shoulders careful to avoid the wound.

"Armand?," she was on her knees beside him.

"I'm fine. We have to get you out of here."

"You're wound," Amelia motioned toward the gash and gasped when she noted the blood had started to congeal and beginning to heal around the edges.

"It's fine," he slowly stood pulling her up, "let's go."

"No, I'm not going with you." Her eyes were watery and large.

"No, you have to come with me!" he was nearly shouting as he shook her by the upper arms.

She pushed him hard causing him to stumble backwards and ran. Amelia had barely made it to the tree line when she felt a body against hers and arms envelop her as she fell to the ground.

"Let me go!" she screamed kicking and clawing at his arms. Armand did as she wished and quickly stood.

"You killed him." She stared at him wide eyed.

"I had to, it was him or us Amelia. Sometimes that happens," he spoke between gasps of air.

"Who is Danielle? And why does that name keep coming up Armand? Was it true what he said? Did you kill her?"

She was still pointing toward the cabin where Cain's lifeless body lay.

He returned her gaze.

His eyes large Armand wasn't sure how to answer her. He had told everyone his father, mother, and even Caesar and Hera that he hadn't killed the girl. But he wasn't sure. He quickly sought an explanation something that would quell her fear. The emotion radiated off her naked body in waves and he felt disgusted that he had caused this.

I'm not sure," he took a step towards her, and she moved back bumping against a tree.

She held up a bloody hand, "no, don't. I don't want you near me."

"Amelia please," he begged as he slowly sunk to his knees.

"It's true. I don't remember her name nor what happened, but I didn't kill her. I couldn't have. I'm," he trailed off sighing as he looked away.

"I didn't kill her. I can't prove it. She came we talked about Cain and how afraid of him she was but, I just brushed her off then she left. I'm not even sure how she got back in the apartment that night nor what exactly happened. I panicked and I ran. That's what I have done Amelia. When things get tough, I call my father and I run. It's always been that way."

He paused watching her. She hadn't ran which gave him hope and he continued. This was a first, but he was willing to bare his soul for her.

"Until you. When I got that photo of you tied up I thought my heart had been ripped out of my chest."

"I assure you I'm not a killer but for you I will kill, and I have. Anyone that's hurts you or threatens you or comes between us I will eliminate. You are my mate; you are everything to me."

She stared at him, her want for him was at an all-time high and she wanted to beat down the sexual monster he had awakened.

His was on his knees with head bowed; she had never had a man submit to her. She never knew she was capable of such and slowly approached him. Once the distance had been closed, she joined him on the ground placing both hands on the sides of his face.

"I believe you; I don't know why but I do."

He placed his arms around her pulling her close.

"I don't want to lose you. I can't lose you. Don't rescind my claim; I would die."

"I am not going to refuse you. I don't think I could. Not now, not ever."

She whispered as her lips touched his. Armand took the lead lying her down on the ground as his body covered hers.

Norman had watched from his post waiting on Cain to emerge and grunted when Amelia came out followed by Armand.

He sent a quick text to Caesar letting him know that his brother was still alive and well.

Caesar had been livid when the message came through showing Evelyn the bad news as she finished dressing.

The pair sat staring at each other Evelyn's arms crossed and a look of disdain on her keen features. Caesar sat in his office chair leg crossed over his right thigh the cell to his chin.

"Plan B?"

He shook his head, "Plan B."

ARMAND WOKE TO SOMETHING sticky, and the scent of blood overpowered him contributing to the blinding headache. He felt a weight

against his side and shifted causing the body on top of him to fall onto the bed.

He screamed the large eyes of the woman fixed on his. It was Danielle and the wound extended from one ear to the other the contents that gave it her long neck structure was gone. The young man had never seen such a sight and scrambled from the bed falling to the floor.

Armand tried to stand but slipped on the pool of blood. He was now covered and began to hyperventilate.

He looked up to see Cain standing in the doorway. Armand was confused as the man wore a smirk.

His mood shifted from fear to anger.

"You did this!"

"No, Armand," he pointed at the body, "this is your fault, had you stayed away this would not have happened!" He shouted.

Armand changed lounging at Cain. The paintings on the wall rattled and shook as they crashed to the floor. Loud banging shook the front door.

"Is everything alright Mr. DuBois, Mr. Lewis?" More banging followed by the door creaking then giving way as someone forced their way in.

Someone shrieks causing the two boys to break apart. Cain in the far corner crouched down sobbing. Armand still dazed and confused the dreadful feeling of a hangover crashing into causing him to be unsteady.

He was near the body in the large puddle of blood he scrambled for something to cover himself as footsteps approached.

What the neighbors saw was something akin to a mad man. The body of Danielle and the bloodied face of Cain.

"He did this! He killed my girlfriend!" Cain screamed running toward them and collapsing as he got near the small crowd. He was caught before his knees touched the floor.

Armand sat up the sheet stuck to his chest. Amelia sat up beside him slowly she placed her arms around her love comforting him as he fought for air.

"It was Cain, all this time," he whispered still attempting to catch his breath, "it was him."

She brought her hand to his chin turning guiding his head so that Amelia could lock eyes with him.

"Breath." The command was spoken softly, and he did as instructed fisting the sheets to prevent his shaking. He felt weak enough without adding a panic attack to the fray.

Slowly, Armand was able to command his breathing puffs of air exiting circular lips in evenly spaced intervals.

"It doesn't matter, he's gone. You're here. You and I are all that matter. I meant what I said earlier. I believe you and I will be by your side always."

He sighed nodding. The heir looked away afraid the vulnerability in his eyes would be met with judgement and disdain. He quickly reminded the inner wounded child that his father wasn't here, and Amelia wasn't his mother advocating on his behalf reminding the man that sired him he was real not and not an idea of an heir.

Amelia pulled him down into her arms and covered them. Soon she was asleep, and Armand listened to the steady rhythm of her heart as it lulled him to sleep.

The Engagement Dinner

The beauty of the space couldn't distract from the bitterness of Cain's blood lingering on his tongue. It was something that no amount of brushing could distort. The liquor only seemed to enhance the taste making him gag after a glass of his finest whiskey.

White flowers were placed over the tables and there was several baby's breath hanging from the ornate chandeliers. The guest entered some of the younger girls oohing their mouths slightly agape. Several of the young woman walked in their lips upturned at not being on the arm of Armand.

The couple and their parents had arrived forty minutes early. His mother insisted they had to preview the décor and made last minute changes. The planner left in a sweat rallying her team to make the changes before the first guest arrived.

All Tina had given him was placed in his safe deposit box. It laid out everything painting a picture of his old man that he didn't want to believe but knew better than to doubt the proof. His father had always been an ambitious man, ruthless. Naively, Armand believed his father had a limit but based on what he had held in his hands a few nights before, the man didn't.

He spotted his parents at the bar. His mother berating a waiter for a crooked bow tie. His father watching amused a slight smirk on his face as he brought the glass of brown liquid to his lips.

Armand approached them slowly his mother smiling at him before she reached for his tie. She mumbled something under her breath, and he couldn't resist rolling his eyes.

"There, that's better."

She brushed his shoulder her lips downturned as she mumbled under her breath again.

"Mother please, I need to speak with Father."

Hemesh dropped her hand stepping back slightly offended, but it was quickly forgotten when she noticed one of the party coordinator's assistants shifting a flower arrangement. The older woman rushed off in a huff causing Armand and Maximillian to share a laugh.

"She loves this stuff." Maximillian stated chuckling, Armand nodded his smile faltering and the lighthearted moment fading.

Maximillian picked up on the shift and placed his glass on the bar.

"Is everything alright son?"

He sighed, feeling like more of a fool. "Did you know? When I told you about the letters and threats against Amelia, did you know beforehand?"

Dark blonde eyebrows went to his forehead, and he looked around.

"Why would you ask that here?" His look was stern but Armand held his gaze.

"Father, we need to talk." He stated leaving no room for dismissal.

Maximillian was tired, there were too many bodies now. His hands were tied, this mystery person was closing in, his illness getting the best of him, but he had enough will to fight this threat against his family.

He didn't have enough to fight his son as well.

"Can we discuss this later? This is your engagement party."

Armand cut him off with one name.

"Samuel Wiltshire," the name was whispered like a song and reflexively his father bristled.

"If we must. Lead the way."

The two men left heading toward the elevators. Hemesh watched her son and husband and could only speculate it wasn't good. She was aware of the threats knowing more than her husband revealed thanks to a letter she had received of her own. All their secrets were at risk of being exposed.

Hers would destroy her marriage.

Armand could feel the early stages of the shift. He closed his eyes attempting to suppress it. It made sense now the push toward Amelia his mother's meddling, Diane's interference. It was a game, a payment for their fathers' misdeeds. It was unfair to Amelia and to him.

"You don't understand son. He was not good for the coven. So, we did what needed to be done."

Armand rolled his eyes, "there is a hell of difference between disagreeing with the alpha and murdering one!" He shouted disgusted by his father's admission.

Knowing Charles conspired with his father to poison Samuel and his father delivered the killing blow turned his stomach.

"The others have to know. They have to know what happened." Armand tried to leave but was stopped by Maximillian.

"Are you stupid? They would kill all of us! Do you want that for your mother, your brother and sister? They would rip all of us apart including you," he whispered harshly gripping his son by the shoulders.

"Why even tell me?" Armand searched his father's eyes.

"Because we need you to choose Amelia. She must be your bride. You have feelings for her and you've already claimed her as your mate. What's the problem?"

There was a long pause before Armand finally spoke.

"It...it isn't right. She doesn't deserve to be tricked and neither did I. How could you do something like this?"

Maximillian chuckled, "do something like this? It isn't right? No one tricked you son." His father mocked before his shoulders shook as laughter boomed and bounced off of the glass.

"You are one to talk!" he shouted at Armand causing him to reflexively recoil. "I know what you did to that girl."

Armand's face fell. "I don't remember it happening. I woke up and she was just there, dead. I..." he trailed off he didn't know what to say.

"Really? By Cain's account you pursued the girl. What was her name by the way? You don't remember, do you? I surely can; shelled out a hell of a lot of money to make her family go away and her friends stop asking questions."

His stomach twisted in a knot he didn't remember her name until the photo and even then her face drew a blank. If it was not for his encounter with Cain he wouldn't have known. It dawned on him that he never knew the names of any of the women he bedded. They were replaceable and he only knew Camille's name because they had grown up together.

Otherwise, her beautiful face would have faded into the background just like the others.

He shook his head gathering the anger he had from before, "it's not the same. I didn't do anything. Cain admitted everything before," he trailed off still not comfortable with what he had to do even if it was to protect his love.

Armand could see the hair starting to bristle on his lower jaw. His father was fighting the shift.

"Killed him, are those the words you're searching for? Luckily for you John was the one that found his body in the cabin and not one of the surveyors. All these years and I am still cleaning up your shit! Now, when it came to Samuel what the fuck do you think I was doing?"

"No, what you did was murder?"

"And you think biting a girl's throat out wasn't? How quickly we forget. Boy, where did we go wrong with you?" Maximillian whispered.

"I just told you I didn't do that. It was Cain."

"I don't know that for sure. You could have made that up to cover up killing the only person that knew the truth. But what I do know is the aftermath that followed and the lengths your mother and I had to go through to clean up your mess. We have cleaned up after you for years now, and how do you repay us? You run off to Spain for six years. Being reckless and sleeping with members of the Spanish Coven. Look here son, I don't mind you being a killer, at least that would make you something, but don't be stupid boy."

Hemesh walked in to find her husband and eldest in a standoff. Both were on the verge of the change, and she quickly closed the door thankful that all of the building had been outfitted with sound proofing when they took over.

"What is all this noise? The guests are starting to arrive." She stated panicked as she looked from her husband to her son.

Armand turned to his mother.

"I won't sit at the table with a murderer." He whispered. Hemesh was taken aback and stared at her husband.

"You told him?"

Armand bristled.

"He already knew Hem. I wanted to make sure he understood. The threats are starting to close in on all of us. He needed to know the true story. Our son needed to know our origins," Maximillian stood up straighter under the intense brown gaze of his wife, "as well as what he must do."

Armand turned to his mother, "you knew about this?"

Hemesh approached him and took his hands in hers.

"Yes, of course, but son, you don't understand how bad things were. If it weren't for your father, the Coven would no longer exist. Your father was well within his right to challenge."

"No, Mother that wasn't a challenge it was a set up."

Amelia entered to find her fiancée and future in laws in a tense standoff.

"Is everything ok?" She asked looking at Armand quickly going to him and placing her hand on his arm.

"No," his eyes had shifted, and Amelia recoiled as she removed her hand. She hadn't witnessed the fury in his eyes since the cabin. She wondered should she have heeded her aunt's warnings.

"Did you know? Have you been playing me like everyone else?" He asked his hard gaze burying into Amelia's; the woman returned his gaze confused.

"What are you talking about, Armand you're scaring me, and you aren't making any sense."

He turned pointing at his father, "my dad and yours poisoned and murdered the former alpha."

"What!" She looked horrified at the bit of information.

There was a loud banging on the door before it opened revealing Caesar.

"The guests are settling in I had the servants extend the cocktail hour since there seems to be some delay. Evelyn is with them keeping the hyenas at bay if you will." He stated somewhat amused.

"Besides, what in the hell is going on here anyway? As usual I wasn't invited to the party." He stated jokingly as he folded his arms noticing the tension.

"Just new revelations brother. Our dad is a killer."

Caesar rolled dark hazel eyes, "and what alpha isn't?" He asked nonchalant staring at Armand.

The eldest brother stood shocked, "what? What is that to say? We have to be exemplary we set the tone for the Coven and every wolf that has conceded to our rule."

Caesar sighed approaching the shell-shocked man placing his hands on his shoulders.

"You are talking about this Samuel thing."

Armand stepped out of his younger brother's grip, "why are you so blasé about this? Our laws have been violated."

Caesar chuckled putting distance between the two.

He stopped looking at Armand, "Really, you want to talk about violating laws. Have you forgotten Danielle, Cain?" He stepped away from his brother and approached his father stopping just only inches from him.

"I told you he wasn't ready. It should be me even he thinks so." He stated pointing at Armand.

Maximillian sighed his gaze for the first time that evening falling on his second born, "you know that is not the proper order of things."

Caesar laughed.

"You two and the 'proper' order of things. I have done everything you wanted. I am going to marry the woman you picked and still I am second fiddle to the screw up. Why? Because he was born first?"

His features were becoming angular, hard and Armand positioned himself ready to protect his mother and Amelia if needed.

Hemesh went to her youngest son and placed her hands on the side of face.

"Son, not now."

Caesar sighed his face softening into those devilish boyish features he had become known for once again. He was sad his eyes becoming iridescent puddles.

"Then when, Mother?"

Hemesh's cheeks were damp.

She knew his pain and frustration and during her children's youth had fought her husband on Caesar and Hera's behalf. She wouldn't allow their upbringing to mirror her own where she was often relegated to the background. It was clear she had failed.

"I don't know son, but our ways and as latter borns we have our place. It is to obey and serve the eldest for the good of our clan and the Coven. Your brother," her dark chocolate gaze rested on her eldest and Armand didn't know eyes could get even sadder.

He had never seen the darkness exhibited today from his brother, nor the despair in his mother. Even Amelia had grown fearful of him, and he wondered how it had come to this.

She turned to her husband, "this is your fault; fix this."

"Armand, you will take over as planned, you and Amelia," for the first time since entering the room she acknowledged Amelia. The younger woman's eyes were wide as she watched the scene unfold.

"I don't think I can do this," Amelia whispered looking at Armand.

He was just as confused as she his gaze on the floor, but he understood if she didn't want to proceed with the union.

Hemesh approached her and took the young woman's hands in her own, "yes you can. Both of you will do this." She turned her hand outstretched for her son, "Armand."

He hesitated briefly before stepping closer and taking his mother's hand. Hemesh placed her son's hand in Amelia's.

"You two are the future. What was done in the past is done? This arrangement will be seen through your mother and father Amelia are just as invested in this as we are. If this fails, the Coven fails, and I will not have our ways end with my bloodline."

"Do you both understand?"

Amelia looked from Armand to her future mother-in-law the older woman's brown eyes bore into hers. She was torn. Her gaze slowly rose to Armand's.

"Do you want this, Armand?" She whispered the question her eyes pleading with his for guidance.

"We must do what is good for the Coven." His voice was strong the tone reassuring.

His hands fell from theirs. "Let's get back to the engagement dinner shall we."

He stood up straighter his shoulders back. Maximillian visibly relaxed offering a small smile. For him, it was over.

"That's it?" Caesar asked his arms folded.

"Yes, there's nothing more the matter is settled, your brother has agreed, and we will support him. You and Evelyn." Max stated.

Caesar laughed, it was dark and low causing the hair on Armand's arms to uncurl becoming soft thorns.

"You think all of this just happened? Camille, Cain, the upheaval on the council. No father, I made it happen."

Hemesh stepped closer, "what are you saying?" She whispered.

Amelia moved to stand next to Armand he pulled her closer wrapping her in a tone armed.

"I am the one responsible for tipping over this house of cards. The threats, the packages, everything that has happened isn't some outside rogues trying to extort money. This is about power. You," he pointed at his father, "are an illegitimate ruler and you, Armand, are unfit to lead."

"Traitor!" His father hissed.

"No father, you are the traitor and murderer, and given how easy it was to find all of the information I needed not a very good one. Next time kill all of the loose ends Father do a better job of burying the evidence."

His skin had taken on a sickly hue, his eyes becoming manic. The change in his appearance even unnerved Maximillian. He knew his children knew their strengths had protected their darkness, but he had never seen this side of his youngest son.

"Caesar," Hemesh tried to approach find a way to cage the animal that was dying to get out, but he simply held up his hand.

"No, Mother, you are not innocent in all of this either. Samira," he looked at his father.

"Did you know that Aunt Samira was pregnant? Ah," he brought his hand to his head in mock forgetfulness, "of course you do. I sent you the report for the autopsy I had done. She was stabbed to death, and I was shocked to learn that evidence was found at the scene and the officer was paid off to keep, oh let's say, a man's Yale shirt being found wrapped around her body suppressed. I wonder why?" he thumped his index finger against his chin.

"I didn't kill Samira," Maximillian whispered.

Caesar sighed, "you are no fun, I know you didn't," he turned around pointing at Hemesh, "she did."

He chuckled giddy at revealing this devastating piece of information.

Maximillian approached his wife his eyes watery, "is this true? Tell me he's lying."

She stared at him her eyes a dark red, "Yes, it's true."

"Why?" He whispered.

"You know why. Because of you. You were the wedge between me and Samira, and she was the ghost between you and me for all these years. When she told me that she was carrying your child I accepted; it wasn't a big deal. I could have lived with that. But then she threaten to tell you and take you away from me and Armand I couldn't let that happen."

"Who is this person? Hemesh?" Maximillian looked at her in horror.

"You didn't see me. You never did. It was always Samira or Samuel that occupied your mind. I figured that if I got rid of her, and you got rid of him that you would finally be mine. That's all I ever wanted."

"Had I known this I would have left you where I found you." His features shifted and so did Hemesh's. She had played a losing game the majority of her adult life. She wouldn't let him win; she wouldn't let the only man she had ever loved leave.

"We are done," he hissed. As Hemesh reached for him, he stepped out of her reach causing her to stumble. Hurt flashed across her face as she brought her hands to her sides.

"The only reason I am letting you live right now is because you are the mother of my children, and I would hate to hurt them further by killing their mother."

He turned walking away.

Hemesh's heart fluttered as she gasped, her world rested on the shoulders of this man and now it was being knocked from its axis. Her Atlas had shrugged.

Out of habit she brought her hand to the perfectly coiffed head of hair and rested on the large sapphire pin. He had barely placed his hand on the doorknob when a groan followed quickly by a gasped echoed in the large space.

Hemesh had moved like lightening and brought the hair pin down into the side of his neck piercing the juggler. He turned grabbing her by the throat, but the blow had been too much for the already weakened man. Slowly, she guided him to the floor with him bleeding against her chest.

Amelia screamed, Armand had moved to stop his mother and growled in frustration when he realized he hadn't been quick enough to stop her.

Caesar merely stood the giddiness from earlier gone replaced by a demented glee.

Armand slowly kneeled beside his parents unsure of what to do as he watched his mother cradle his father's head against her body slightly rocking back and forth. He was weak and Armand could only hear the apology his father whispered against his mother's breast.

The words stopped as Maximillian went limp and from the shaking of his mother's shoulders he knew his father was gone.

"Mother?" Armand whispered placing a hand on her shoulder.

"I can't live without him," she took a deep breath, "I won't live without him."

He screamed as he watched her plunged the same hairpin in the side of neck her eyes went large before they quickly closed. She held back the pain as she had done for many years. Hemesh pulled Maximillian's body closer as she slowly began to slouch forward.

Armand fell backward his heart pounding he wasn't sure what to do and wanted to ram his head against the floor. Part of him wanted to rip out Caesar's heart for opening of covered wounds and ushering in the destruction of their world.

Laughter echoed around him, and he looked up to see his brother gripping his sides bent over.

"Now brother," he stood up straight speaking between laughs, "that was better than any tragedy Sophocles could have whipped up."

He clapped and Armand stood his blood boiling.

Caesar stopped staring at his brother before looking around the room and pointing at himself, "you mad at me bro?" he asked mockingly.

"You did all of this."

"No, they did all of this, I merely pointed it out. Now, just think, a couple of questions here and there and bam some college kid doing a report on folklore would have found this. Be thankful. With the exception of her father," he nodded in Amelia's direction, "everyone tied to this thing, this regicide is gone, dead. Now, you can try and be king." He placed his hands in his pockets.

"If you got the guts."

"Our parents are dead. What are we going to tell Hera?," he paused watching his young brother, "how can you live with yourself?"

He pinched the bridge of his nose, "that's why I have been telling father, or rather had been, telling father that you are unfit. Too emotional, asking too many questions about my feelings. Hera will be well in due time. Tell her she has full access to her trust fund, and you'll find out how quickly the grieving process will be over. I swear that girl blows through money quicker than you do women. Or rather used to do women."

He looked at Amelia wiggling his eyebrows, "you got him all on lock now. You and your emotional train wreck over there."

He shook his head whispering under his breath, "Evelyn and I could do this in our sleep."

"You won't get the chance?" Armand shed his clothes hair multiplying over his body.

Caesar chuckled as he did the same, "I've been waiting a long time for this brother."

Amelia rushed to the wall to steer clear of the battle raging before her, and just like with Cain she feared for Armand's life. He was still weak from the injuries suffered at the cabin.

Caesar latched onto Armand's arm causing him to howl in pain as he tore away flesh there exposing muscle. The older DuBois brought his large paw across the younger's face blinding him in one eye.

The two parted fangs bloody fur matted to their bodies as the forms of scarred men appeared.

Caesar immediately brought his hand up to cover the exposed right socket; the eye lying ten feet from him.

"I'm going to kill you," he hissed. Caesar whipped around to face Amelia, "then you're next."

"I wouldn't think about it if I were you."

He laughed his face shifting as the jaw drop elongating, Armand went through a similar transformation and the hairs on Amelia's arms stood up.

Armand lunged first catching his brother on the back leg. He howled in pain before swiping a paw across Armand's face causing the larger wolf to release him.

Amelia hadn't heard a door open but screamed when the sound of a gunshot reverberated throughout the room.

Evenly stood near the door the Glock pointed at the pair. Amelia followed Evelyn's gaze to Armand he was on his side coiled in a ball as fur slowly receded giving way to tan flesh.

Caesar took on his human form staggering as he approached Evelyn.

"Good shot babe," he spoke through bloodied teeth.

Evelyn turned the gun on Amelia, "what about her?"

"Well, she knows everything now. I suppose we have to kill her too." He wiped at the blood that had pooled at the corners of his mouth.

Evelyn paused smirk on her face.

"With pleasure," Evelyn moved to pull the trigger and with lightning speed Amelia moved sticking close to the wall as she headed toward the door opposite the pair.

"Fuck!" Evelyn screamed as she emptied the clip.

"How did she move so fast?" She was breathless as she lowered the gun.

Caesar wobbled as he reached for Evelyn.

"Forget her for now. Once I become alpha we will have all the resources at our disposal to find her."

Evenly placed the gun in her purse.

"Let's get downstairs, I think the carnage here is enough to make our claims. Cain ambushed your mother and father, Armand tried to intervene but was overpowered."

He smiled placing a firm kiss on her lips.

"That's right babe. Not yet. One thing." He pulled away from her unsteady and approached Armand.

Roughly he took Armand's shoulder and rolled him over causing his brother to yell in pain. Caesar dug into the wound causing the older DuBois to wiggle and grunt as he plunged his fingers in further. With a quick jerk he ripped the bullet from the wound taking bits of flesh with it.

"There you piece of shit! You were never fit to lead and when I find Amelia I am going to rip out her fucking heart! I'll be sure to bury all of you together." He hissed standing.

"Let's go, he'll bleed out by time we get back," he turned to Evelyn. She met him halfway wrapping her arms around his waist.

A New Era

Amelia waited underneath the stairs digging in her claws and using a spell her aunt had taught her. Their voices no longer traveled, and she heard shuffling along with a door slam.

She moved as mist and transformed into wolf form as she entered the room figuring she would be better able to protect herself. She found Armand slowly dragging himself toward the door a long trail of blood behind him.

She rushed over to him; Armand attempted to reach for her but his arms fell with a thud against the floor and he groaned as more blood gushed from the wounds. Amelia sensed her love didn't have much time and crouched lower her belly on the floor as she offered him her back.

Catching her meaning, he hissed as he moved quickly shifting onto her back as he wrapped both arms around her neck. She moved barely giving him enough time to get settled. Armand held on tight as she increased her pace. Both heard the sound of hurried footsteps.

She hopped down a flight at a time and soon they were at the bottom. Amelia paused spotting her parents they seemed worried but given that her father was a part of Maximillian's scheme she decided against going to him for help and instead moved toward an exit door.

The young woman focused whispering another spell causing the door to open wide enough for the pair to make their escape.

She snaked her way down an alley stepping over a sleeping homeless man with a bottle clutched against his chest. She needed to get them someone fast Armand was fading and with the amount of blood he lost she wasn't sure how long he would last.

SEVERAL PARTY ATTENDEES screamed. The anger at having to wait forgotten as a bloodied Caesar slumped against Evelyn came into view.

"Help please!" Evelyn cried out as the two collapsed several members crowding around them.

Charles and Diane shoved several people out of the way to get to the couple.

"What happened? Caesar?" Charles crouched down beside the young man. Hera quickly joined them her eyes watery as she looked around.

"Where's Mother? Father?" she reached for his hand her eyes locked on Evelyn.

Evelyn shook her head, "I'm sorry. It was an ambush, I only caught the end of it," she turned to her fiance placing her hand on his forehead.

"It was Armand! He's insane. He attacked Father, Mother tried to stop them, oh my God," he cried out, "I did my best, but I was too late."

A look of confusion passed over Evelyn's face, but she quickly schooled her features her expressing concern over her intended. She would discuss with Caesar this change in plan as she was unsure of how they would sell it, but it was too late; tales of an ambush were forgotten, Armand would be the culprit.

"My daughter? Amelia!?" Charles shouted looking around.

"She wasn't there, I don't know what happened to her. Please, upstairs, my parents." He pointed letting his hand fall as he fell backwards.

"Get him to a hospital," Charles barked the order and ran for the stairwell. He would get their faster than by elevator. He needed to find his daughter.

Charles entered the room to find blood everywhere and his friend of over forty years dead on the floor. He closed his eyes breathing deep. Something didn't feel right he could sense his daughter was still alive, but he doubted if Armand would do all of this. He approached the trail of blood and bent down to gather some on his fingertips.

It was Armand's quickly he pulled his handkerchief gathering more blood and tucked the cloth in his pocket. He would pay Maxine a visit.

Three scouts entered looking around. They paused at the body of their alpha all three lowered themselves to one knee and bowed their heads.

"Clean this up, take their bodies to the sanctuary. I will exam them later."

EVELYN DISMISSED THE councilmen that stood around the hospital bed. She waited nearly twenty minutes before she spoke wanting to be sure no one was lurking.

"Why the change in plan?"

Caesar held up his hand, she took it taking a seat on the bed beside him.

"I know it was impulsive, but it further strengthens my claim as alpha if I paint him as a madman, and besides it works better in our favor."

"He wasn't there. Somehow he escaped; they didn't find his body."

"All the more reason he has to be painted as a mad man. Before his death my father named him alpha and if he is simple missing I wouldn't be able to move at all until he was found. The council would take control but with my brother now a fugitive in the deaths of my parents I am the next heir."

She smiled the plan becoming clear as she placed his hand on her lower abdomen.

His unbandaged eye bulged slightly when he squeezed the firm round flesh.

"I was going to wait until after the party, but I'm pregnant," she spoke softly.

"Wow, this is truly a new beginning for us all." He smiled lightly stroking her belly with his thumb.

The lithe blond entered with the three scouts.

"Any luck?"

"No sir." They all looked down disappointed.

"Keep searching. I have to bring my brother to justice. I..." he trailed off making sure to look solemn, "I don't know how to console my sister. I don't know what to tell her. I can only offer her justice. Now go!"

They nodded in unison leaving their new alpha.

He motioned for Norman to come closer. The slender young man leaned forward his ear hovering near Caesar's mouth.

"Find Amelia and Armand. Kill them both."

The smile that spread across Norman's face was sinister as he stood giving Caesar a slight nod before departing.

WEEKS PASSED SINCE the deaths of Maximillian and Hemesh spread like a wildfire and Caesar received many gifts of condolences from the other covens. The perceived murders of his parents only aided in his push for the League.

He stood before the council many of the members sat stone faced several did not hide their disdain for him or the ideas that he would be shortly implementing.

"With the murder of my father, your alpha, by our own, my sister and I are orphans, and the Coven has been robbed of an alpha in his prime. Not only that but my father and mother were robbed of the chance to ever see the birth of their first grandchild. But with tragedy comes opportunity. An opportunity to begin anew."

"Gentlemen, as your alpha I will lead us into this new era and my first order as the head of this Coven will be to hunt down my brother so we may bring him to justice.

About the Author

Hayley M. Moon is an Alabama native and *Taming Armand Book 1 of the Coven Origins Series* is her debut novel. Hayley is the author of horror, science fiction and noir short stories. She manages her blog *The Weirdo Writes.* When she's not writing or daydreaming she's crocheting and hoarding books.

Read more at hayleymoon.com.